ROWAN EDWARDS

THIS HEART OF STONE

Complete and Unabridged

LINFORD
Leicester

First published in Great Britain in 1994 by
Robert Hale Limited
London

First Linford Edition
published December 1995
by arrangement with
Robert Hale Limited
London

British Library CIP Data

Edwards, Rowan
This heart of stone.—Large print ed.—
Linford romance library
I. Title II. Series
823.914 [F]

ISBN 0-7089-7791-X

Published by
F. A. Thorpe (Publishing) Ltd.
Anstey, Leicestershire

Set by Words & Graphics Ltd.
Anstey, Leicestershire
Printed and bound in Great Britain by
T. J. Press (Padstow) Ltd., Padstow, Cornwall

This book is printed on acid-free paper

Love and peace to Liam and Adam
(the new Woodstock generation)

THIS HEART OF STONE

Beatrice's coolly ordered English life erupted into chaos when she learned of her parents' secret — successfully kept for twenty-one years. Shocked, angry, determined to uncover her own roots, she headed for America — to Brooklyn. Here, her search led to reclusive sculptor, Mal Cameron, the only known link with her mother's mysterious past. But what exactly was that link; just how deep did it go and did she really want to find out?

Books by Rowan Edwards
in the Linford Romance Library:

WHERE THE HEART IS
SWEET VENGEANCE
ISLAND MAGIC

1

"WHEN among wolves, you have to howl."

Where had Beatrice read this nugget of advice? Most likely in one of the dozens of books she'd dutifully engulfed, during these past three years. It echoed back to her mind now, with a hollow precision.

Only hours since stepping on to American soil, shuffling through Customs at Kennedy Airport along with the travel-weary herd, already it was getting to her. Within minutes she'd been *have-a-nice-day*-ing as if to the manner born. Flight attendants, ground staff, immigration officials, the young woman on the hire-car firm's desk . . .

Fixing up the hire of this vehicle had been simplicity itself. The uniformed clerk had combined crisp efficiency with a direct approachability rarely found in equivalent British circumstances.

"Your first visit to the States, Miss Cole?"

"That's right."

"You have friends here? Or family?"

"Sort of."

"Do you have far to drive, Ma'am?"

"Not really," Beatrice had said. "I'm heading upstate; Woodstock."

"Ah, it's great up there! You'll love it. The British always do."

You don't say? Beatrice had thought; but she only said: "Do they?"

The young woman had stamped a form, then surveyed Beatrice over the top of her driving licence. "Driven on the right before, Miss Cole?"

"As a matter of fact, I haven't. But don't worry," Beatrice had assured her, "I'm a competent driver. Four years, and an unblemished record. I'll be fine."

"Sure you will." The clerk handed Beatrice her licence. "I was only thinking, it takes extra concentration, and you must be bushed after your flight. Why not rest up a while before you head through the city?"

Beatrice had fought off the usual paranoid twinges. This woman couldn't have been more than a couple of years older than herself. But she wasn't criticising; her interference wasn't even personal, merely routine concern for her firm's car.

"I'll have something to eat, and sit for an hour before I leave. Don't worry," Beatrice repeated, "your Datsun will be safe in my hands."

The symmetrical smile had shifted gear, just a fraction, but from fixed to manual. "I won't worry, Miss Cole — as long as you don't." The clerk opened a map of New York State, which looked peculiarly sparse; then another of New York City, which looked intimidatingly crammed. "Now, let's see how we can best help you plan your getaway."

Beatrice's normal pride and independence had crumpled in the face of such amiable charm, and her own exhaustion. Gratefully, summoning her last shreds of mental energy, she had noted the young woman's sensible directions, arranging when and where to pick up the car. Then she had meekly obeyed the expert lecture about resting up before driving.

Beatrice's experience of airports was far from wide, but in her opinion, this arrivals lounge was sleazy. And she still hadn't recovered from the interminable queue at Immigration. Lines of zomboid travellers, bleary from their journey, waiting patiently to get their documents checked; and at seven in the morning, local time. What was that — midday, British time?

She had watched the American citizens marching through their own channel, with minimal fuss. Here, Beatrice and her British passport were alien; here, she was an outsider — a new role, only serving to heighten her inbuilt defence mechanisms.

Later, refreshed and optimistic, she

had hit the trail, assorted maps spread beside her. Her reflexes had always been quick, and driving on the right proved no problem. But coping with the maze of New York traffic was something else. At a glance, these were the fastest, craziest, dirtiest streets she'd seen, anywhere. Probably the meanest, too, if you were foolhardy enough to emerge from the safety of your moving steel container.

Signs to Harlem, the Bronx; over there, a glimpse of the — not just the, but *the* — famous Manhattan skyline? But Beatrice dared not take a proper look. She needed all her wits to negotiate this route.

Anyway, she wasn't here for the sightseeing. She wasn't your average tourist. She had a private mission, a goal; nothing must distract her.

Mercifully, the desk clerk's directions stayed in her mind, and the road-signs were lucid. Eventually Beatrice found herself crossing one more choked bridge, roaring through one more fumey underpass, over yet another, wider bridge — and suddenly released out of that mayhem, on a highway bordered with green, which skirted invisible suburbs, following the broad, beautiful Hudson river.

The woman had predicted that her getaway would take well over an hour, and it had. Now it was mid-morning, under a glaring July sun. Good news, this air-conditioned car with its tinted windscreen — a change from the battered old VW Beetle she was used to driving at home.

Home! The word, the idea, caused Beatrice a sharp pang — which in turn shocked her. Hadn't she deliberately cultivated this cool self-image, the interior matching the exterior: the original level head, the poised English blonde, always in charge of her responses? But she had to excuse herself a brief lapse. She was very much alone, by anyone's standards, and London seemed a world away. All of, what was it, five thousand miles? Geography had never been her strongest point. Her recently-acquired degree had been in Economics, combined with Psychology. It was part of a master plan, carefully conceived and followed. Beatrice Cole was destined to be the ideal Nineties Woman: pursue a formidable career in hard-headed Business Management, but laced with proper human insights.

She had sat her final exams in the week of her twenty-first birthday, but she had refused to let that ruffle her. She had always, from a small girl, refused to let life ruffle her. She had ambitions, and she was not the woman to see them thwarted by personal considerations.

Was it only a month or so ago, that red-letter day when her excellent results had come through? Looking back on it now, it had been a truly extraordinary day; one of those pivotal points after which everything is irrevocably and inevitably changed.

Lit up with her achievement, that evening she had confronted her proud parents, busy sharing the washing-up, as usual. After breaking the great news, she had added, without preamble, the ultimate bombshell. She intended, she informed them, to continue her studies in the States.

"I've already got a place at New York City University," she had announced. "I didn't want to tell you before, because I had to get a First, to take it up. But now I can definitely go!"

"New York?" Her mother had gone uncharacteristically shrill; then glanced at her father, who had turned noticeably pale. "Why?"

"Because I want to travel. I've always said so, haven't I?"

"But Bea, love, why there?" Her father was ever-reasonable. "When you could go anywhere in the world?"

"Why not? I don't want to go just anywhere; I want to go to America! I want to see New York, explore upstate a bit. I don't really know why — I just have this feeling. I've had it for ages . . . sort of . . . I feel drawn there. Pulled. I don't know . . ." Then Beatrice had faltered, because although her confession was intensely true, it was also fanciful — unexplainable by logic, and therefore slightly dangerous.

Her mother had stared hard at her — puzzled, agitated, even for her mother. "Why *there*?" she had persisted. "Of all . . ."

"Look, Mum, I thought you'd be pleased! It hasn't been easy, you know — I had to have astronomical grades all along the line, then glowing references from all the top . . ."

"I know, darling," her mother had interrupted, in a tight, cracked voice. "You've done brilliantly. We know how hard you've worked. It's just that . . ."

"Just that what?" Beatrice had glared from one dazed parental face to the other. "If it's the money, you needn't worry; I'll be independent, they've given me a bursary, and the fare. I won't be rich, but I've got my generous twenty-first birthday presents, from you and from Grandma. I'll sell my car, and

I can always get a job there to help out; most people have to do that in the States when they're studying. I won't be sponging on you, don't worry."

"It's not that, Bea."

She had looked sharply at her father, and was appalled at what she saw. He seemed stunned; almost ill, as if her news had sent him literally reeling. She might have expected such a dramatic reaction from her mother, but never her father.

"Then what is it, Dad?" Suddenly, she had felt quite frightened, sensing, yet not understanding, their mutual alarm — not far short of panic. "I really want to go. They run this special postgraduate . . ."

"Of course, Beatrice. Of course you must go. It's wonderful news." Typically, her mother was pulling herself together. Judith Cole lapsed only too easily into frenzied anxiety, but she had amazing powers of recovery. Her husband might seem to take traumas on the chin; but underneath, in the longer run, he was often the one who caved in. In a close partnership, over two decades and more, they both recognised those subtle balances which the world does not always see. "Mustn't she, Simon?" Judith rounded on him now, as if appealing for permission.

When there was no reply, Beatrice rounded on him too. Both women waited, their eyes fixed on his face. Normally good-natured but bland, that face was registering some turbulent emotions. Still pale, it was working between anger, fear and a supreme effort of control — all three clearly visible to his wife and daughter.

Instinctively, Beatrice ran to seize his arm. She had never seen him like this before. "Dad! What's the matter? Dad!"

"We'll have to tell her," he was mumbling, "I've always told you, Jude . . . I knew she'd . . . we'd . . . it's a judgement . . . we should have . . . "

Judith was shaking her head. "Simon, don't be an idiot! We won't have to.

Why should we? She'll have nothing to do with . . . "

"To do with what? Mum, Dad — *what*?" It was Beatrice's turn to panic. Her throat was dry, her stomach constricted. She knew her mother to be a volatile, expressive woman; but her father never gave way to such open demonstrations. All her life, he had cultivated a distant kindness — a certain aloofness, especially (it seemed) toward Beatrice; in fact she had cultivated a mirror image of it herself, perhaps as a form of self-preservation. Simon was naturally reserved, she often told herself; and yet she had to admit — when she took time out to ponder on such profound realities, which was seldom, despite her academic interest in Psychology — he managed a fluency of contact with her younger brothers and sister which had always been lacking with her.

Now Simon collapsed into a kitchen chair, burying his face in his hands. When he looked up, he was no longer pale, but dark red.

"You'll have to tell her now, Jude," he croaked. "I won't let her go unless you do. God knows what could happen, if she doesn't know the truth!" He shuddered — and without knowing why, so did Beatrice.

"The truth about what? Mum? Dad?"

Judith put an arm round her husband and helped him to his feet. "Come on, Simon — no need to go over the top! All right, we'll tell her, if you think it's so important. It's my responsibility. I'll tell her."

"Of course it's important! Can't you see . . . "

"Yes, yes," she soothed. "I can see. I can see." She guided him to the door. "Go and join the kids in the sitting room — they're watching some quiz show. Or better still, go up and have a bath. That generally helps calm you down. I'll explain everything to Bea, don't worry. It'll be fine. There, that's right. There!"

At the door, Simon had turned back to his daughter. "Don't be angry with us, Bea!" he had implored. "We thought it was best . . . we didn't think you'd ever need to know."

Beatrice had bitten her lip to stay silent as he disappeared, shutting the door behind him. Then she had swung to face her mother, who was leaning against a wall, staring ahead — or perhaps inward.

"Know what, Ma?" Now Beatrice kept her voice carefully subdued. She felt as if she was watching herself, acting in a play. Whatever her parents were so worked up about, it was obviously real enough to them — but there was surely no call for such histrionics?

"Come and sit down, and I'll tell you."

Beatrice had obeyed, and her mother had launched in at once. "Just remember, darling, whatever else you're going to think and feel, about us and about yourself, in these next few minutes — twenty-two years is a long time ago. A heck of a long time."

A heck of a long time. Beatrice's head reverberated the phrase now, a few weeks later, as she drove north on the Thruway. She had tensed all over, re-living those critical minutes. She must relax; loosen up.

This could have been a British motorway, except for being the wrong way round — and more sedate, with a top speed limit of fifty-five, which she was finding it hard to observe. She had never driven with an automatic gearbox before, but it was easy, especially on this sort of road. On and on, straight and straight. Few exits, few stopping places. Not much to see. To be honest, it was dull: she missed the rolling vistas, the fields and urban glimpses of home. Here, there was only this endless scrubland and low, tree-clad hills.

She realised they must be the foothills of the Catskills. She passed a signboard that declared she was heading for Albany and Montreal. Montreal! The immense distances of this country! Albany, the State capital, a hundred miles up the road; and next, Canada! Turn off, if you must, for Poughkeepsie, Kingston, Schenectady, Troy — but be sure and watch for those exit signs, or you'll be stuck on this freeway, have to keep on and on, straight and straight, never a bend or a break . . .

Beatrice forced alertness back to her weary eyes. That hire-car woman had been justified, questioning her fitness for this drive, so soon after the flight. But she was half-way now, and doing fine. At this rate she should be at Woodstock by lunch-time, check in at that Motel the travel agency had told her about, snatch a few hours' rest and be ready for — well, for whatever revelations the next few days might yield.

She yawned and fumbled for the radio switch. Ten minutes later she was considerably wiser about the Hudson Valley news and weather, the contents of certain Hudson Valley stores, the efficiency of selected Hudson Valley businesses, the entertainments showing at the Kingston Mall movie theaters, and the pop numbers currently in the local charts. It seemed the rest of time and space had dwindled to this confined spot. Who needed to know about wider issues, when life in the 'nineties was real, rich and rewarding, right here in the lovely Hudson Valley?

Suddenly, Beatrice felt claustrophobic, here in this cool car; even this six-lane freeway, when she longed to explore the new landscapes tantalisingly tucked behind those steep verges. But then, she reminded herself, the only reliable landscape was her own, inner one. Wherever she went, however far she roamed — in a three-foot cubicle or a boundless plain — she would always be at the hub of it.

Beatrice sighed a philosophical lament for her own limitations. She was so busy sighing, she almost missed the sign off to Saugerties. Thank goodness, a proper road, with twists and gradients! And here were picturesque wooden houses with open front gardens; shops, schools, garages. Ordinary existence had been going on behind the green screen along the Thruway, after all. Thank goodness!

Now Beatrice craved a very wet shower and a very long sleep, in that order. Followed by a very nourishing meal, not served up in airline moulded plastic and fairly indistinguishable from it. After that, she might have the strength to implement Plan A. It was one thing to formulate Plan A in the familiar surroundings of home; another to arrive here and activate it — especially feeling as scruffy as she did now.

But she'd made it! She was here! All at once, it seemed a miracle: her eyes blurred, her chest tightened. Pure exhaustion, that was all. She was on the last lap: she reached to switch on the radio again. "Today's weather," it told her, in genial male tones, "has been brought to you by Hudson Valley Pest Control."

The outskirts of Woodstock took shape, drenched in afternoon sunshine, verdantly serene. The place did not look to Beatrice like a world-famous mecca for fans of nineteen-sixties rock music; it looked like a peaceful small North American town. If it had secrets, for the moment, it guarded them to itself, offering neither questions nor answers. Beatrice fully intended to uncover both.

2

EARLY next morning, when it would be lunch-time in England, Beatrice put in a quick call to Judith.

It was difficult. She had promised to keep in close touch, but she was still bitter. And what was there to say? Everything, and nothing. *Arrived safely. Reasonable flight. Temperature outside 30 centigrade, but motel cool and comfortable. Feeling OK, tell you more later.*

Then she wandered up and down lively Tinker Street, mustering her thoughts and feelings, preparing for action. With her mother inevitably at the forefront of her mind, she bought three transparent window decals: rainbow, black cat, rolling hillside scene. That evening, she followed the phone call up with a written progress report.

Dear Mum, you'll have to excuse this scrawl, she wrote. *This dispatch comes to you direct from Woodstock village green. I'm sitting on a bench, watching people parading past, slurping ice-creams, swigging beer, generally relaxing in a summer-evening sort of way. It seems that old hippies never die, they just retire to Woodstock and tie-dye. I do like this place, Mum; the way all the buildings are made of wood. I don't suppose its changed much since you knew it. I don't know whether all these fancy shops and galleries were here then, but it still seems a genuinely arty-crafty sort of community. No shortage of cash around, though.*

Solly, the motel manager, reckons there's more city dropouts here than natives. He and his family emigrated here from Queens a few years ago. He's full of gems for the discerning visitor. Did you know the first white man arrived here from New York in 1607 and was slaughtered by

Indians forty years later? I listened politely because I wanted to further my researches by pumping him a bit. I started by asking about cheap places to eat. Then I took a deep breath and mentioned this family I knew of, called Byrne, who used to be involved in the art scene, around the time of the Festival. I asked casually if he happened to know if they were still around?

He said he hadn't been here nearly long enough, but if I want to trace anyone like that, there's one man who's sure to know. Been here all his life, some kind of sculptor, name of Malcolm Cameron. I got my Sherlock Holmes hat on and tried his number, which Solly gave me. So far, no problem, only I kept getting his answering machine. I suppose if he's a sculptor he must leave the horrible thing on when he's working. He has this deep intimidating voice, and you know how I hate those machines at the best of times. Twice I lost my nerve and put the phone down, but the third time I thought, this is ridiculous — so I plucked up the nerve and left a message; just my number and my name, but nothing else, so I'm hoping he'll be intrigued enough to call back, but I've hung around most of the afternoon and he hasn't yet. Which is why I'm out now, taking the air. Better get moving — I've got a cramp in my arm, as well as certain other parts from sitting so long.

Beatrice mused for a few minutes, then added:

I know you'd really rather I wasn't doing this, Mum, but I also know you're not surprised, in fact you must understand why I have to. Please give my love to Dad . . .

Beatrice hesitated, crossed out *Dad*, wrote *Simon*; then crossed that out and wrote: *everyone, and don't worry about me, I'll be fine. Much love, Beatrice.*

* * *

Predictably, a telephone message waited in her pigeon hole at the motel. "M. Cameron called, about 8.30 p.m., please call him back."

Crumpling it in her hand, she went to her room. One could go on like this for weeks, playing cat and mouse with answering machines. What time was it now — nine-thirtyish? Too late to try his number again?

No. She had no excuse to put it off till tomorrow. Strike while the will was iron, or something. Neither her energy nor her funds would last forever, especially the latter. She sat on her bed, picked up the receiver and dialled the number. She was beginning to know it by heart.

"Cameron."

This time the voice was real, not recorded; that same sonorous bass, but with added ingredient X: what could she call it, a tough warmth?

"Er, hallo!" she ventured.

"Hi, yes? Can I help you?"

"Is that er, Mr Cameron?" She hated this version of herself, all twittery, but for once in her life, she really couldn't help it.

"Mal Cameron here, yes. Who is this?"

"You don't know me, Mr Cameron, but I'm . . . "

"Beatrice Cole, right?"

"Right." The way he pronounced her surname made it more interesting: broadening it, deepening it, instead of her own prissy narrow 'o'.

"You're English, right?"

"Is it that obvious?"

"Sure it's that obvious! Why — are you ashamed of it or something?"

"Not at all, but I . . . "

"So, Beatrice Cole, to what do I owe this honour? Why would a charming English lady call me up from a motel in downtown Woodstock, and not merely once but three times?"

"How do you know I rang three times? I only left a message once!"

Cameron was manifestly entertained. "In words, sure — but there's messages, and messages. Could it be that you breathe with an accent? Let me tell you, there's something about a British silence that's a whole lot different than an American one."

"Sort of stiff and formal, instead of free and easy?"

"Maybe that's it. So, here I am, in person, no technological barriers. What's the story?"

"The thing is," she said, "I'm visiting the area, and I wanted to try and trace some old friends of my . . . at least, there's this family connection and I wondered if they might still be . . . that is, I was told you might know . . . " Damn! She'd thought she was word-perfect, these lines polished for hours in her head.

"We have someone in common?" he was drawling. "How fascinating! Who could it be? Do I know any English people?"

"Oh, they're not English. Their name is Byrne.

"Byrne? Byrne!" His piercing whistle nearly ruptured her eardrum. "You mean, B-y-r-n-e, as in Bob and Peggy, ran the craft workshops?"

"I think that might be them. Only it wasn't Bob and Peggy my, er, friends knew, it was someone called . . . she faltered, just for a second, "called Jim. It could be the same family."

"You bet it's the same family," Malcolm Cameron assured her. "Jimmy was the oldest son. I was at school with his kid sister, Kerry, the youngest — it was a big family, five or six of 'em. Jim must have been, let me see, twelve, thirteen years older? He'd be . . . " again the ear-splitting whistle, "early forties by now. Wow!"

"Yes," Beatrice replied. "He would be."

"So what did you say your connection with them was, precisely?"

"I didn't, Mr Cameron. Not precisely."

"Okay, okay, Miss Cole. No call to go biting my head off."

"Sorry," she mumbled. She must control her nerves; he sounded temperamental, and she couldn't risk alienating him, not yet, with so much at stake. "It's just someone I knew, who knew this, er, Jim."

"They left Woodstock years back, you realise that?"

"No, I didn't realise." She tried to keep the disappointment from her tone. "Do you happen to know where they went?"

"It's been a tidy few years since anyone asked after the Byrnes. I'd almost forgotten them." There was a pause. "Almost, not quite." Another pause. Beatrice held her peace, and also her breath. "As it happens, I do know where some of them went. Kerry lives on Long Island with husband and a brood, but I haven't heard from her in years. I seem to remember Bob and

Peggy retired to Sun City, Florida. Jim went to New York, became some big cheese in academic circles, you knew that?"

Beatrice's heart thumped so loudly, she was sure he must hear it. "I'm not sure, I . . . "

"Some kind of professor, science, or was it Math?"

"I see." She waited, hoping for further enlightenment. When none was offered, she went on, "I don't want to be a nuisance, Mr Cameron. If you could let me have any addresses you've got, for Kerry, or the parents, I could take it from there and leave you in peace."

"You want to leave me in peace?"

"As I say, I wouldn't want to bother you."

"Bother? It's no bother." He was parodying her clipped English vowels. "No bother at all. But I do reckon one thing, Miss Cole."

She struggled to keep calm. "What's that, Mr Cameron?"

"I think I prefer not to divulge other folks' private details over the phone. Especially not to someone I never met in my life. I think, if you want them so badly, you'll have to collect them from me in person."

"What makes you so sure I want them so badly?"

"Call it a hunch. So how about coming on up here, and we'll see what we can dig out for you?"

"Up where?"

"Where do you think? Where I live."

"When?"

"Whenever you like. Right now, if you're some kind of insomniac. Maybe you won't snatch a wink of sleep till you get this information?"

"I'm not *that* desperate," she asserted. "But I'll come and see you, if that's the most convenient."

"You have a car?"

"A hired one, yes."

"Busy tomorrow?"

Was he joking? Come to think of it, he probably was. "Not really."

"Okay. Come tomorrow, any time. I'll be here all day, working."

"You don't mind daytime visitors when you're working?"

"Not if I've invited them," said Malcolm Cameron. "If I choose not to see or speak to anyone, I just don't. When I'm engaged on a special project, which I am at this moment, I might work through the night. When I decide to stop, then I stop. No one dictates my hours of creation, or recreation. Except me."

"Fair enough." She wondered about his family, if he had one. Such autocratic habits must be hard on them.

"So, you turn up here, whenever you feel like it. Ask that old crook, Solly, for the address. It's easy, you just drive up the hill out of town, past where Bob Dylan used to live . . . along the Ohayo Mountain Road — Solly'll tell you."

Bob Dylan, forsooth! "I'll be there in the morning, Mr Cameron."

"The name is Mal," he snarled.

"You British are so darned formal!"

"Fine," Beatrice said sweetly. "Thanks, then, Mal. I'll see you."

"See you, Beatrice Cole. Have a nice night."

Without knowing his face, she was uncertain whether he was being straight or sarcastic, which worried her. Beatrice liked to have the upper hand in conversations, and more often than not, she got it.

In the morning, she checked the route with Solly. He looked a bit sheepish, as well he might. *M. Cameron called*, indeed! 'That old crook Solly' knew M. Cameron well enough. She could imagine, only too clearly, their exchange, concerning her.

"This English dame, staying at your place, been asking for me. What gives, hey, Solly?"

"Search me, Mal! Didn't even know she was calling you."

"Name of Cole. What's she like? What's she want?"

"Oh, she's trying to trace some

contact. All alone here, doesn't give much away — could be on holiday? Little blonde piece, young — early twenties — pert, petite."

"You'd call her the English Rose type?"

"Not exactly. Not so sweet and gentle. More — you know, sharp."

"Feisty, hey? Well, you leave a message, make sure she gets it."

"I'll tell her to try you again, right?"

"You do that. Make sure you do that, you old bastard."

"Leave it with me, Mal. No problem. I'll see she tries again."

Wooing sleep, Beatrice tried to envisage this Cameron, fit a frame and features to the wry, resonant tones. He had to be big, sounding as he did. Apart from that, she had nothing to build on. Which was why she hated telephones: most useful invention, least normal communication.

Twelve hours later, she was pulling the car up in a driveway, off a steep, tree-lined road. It was one of those individual wooden houses. Round the back, she could see a cleared lawn, bathed in sunshine, and a wide verandah where the rays filtered through. Otherwise the whole place was in dappled shade, a welcome oasis of cool.

She pressed the front door bell. Nothing happened, so she pressed harder. It rang emptily back at her. The house had an empty feeling, altogether. In fact, when she looked carefully, it was unkempt — not entirely the desirable residence it appeared at first glance. Bits were hanging off, splintering, rotting. Evidently M. Cameron was too occupied with whatever he sculpted to attend to the mundane requirements of his beautiful family home. Yes, it was an ideal spot for raising children in — but they were tidily out of sight this morning.

Beatrice walked round the side, across the green pool of sunshine. Intuition led her to an outhouse, nestling among the trees. Low, but rambling, almost as large as the main house. Approaching it, she heard sounds of life. Distinct life: loud energetic activity.

Cameron was a sculptor, so this must be his studio. She banged on the door with both fists; nothing tentative, not too English. Immediately, so that she almost fell in, it was flung open. She caught an instant glimpse of rubble and debris. Massive slabs of white stone, smaller chunks of the same. And some serious equipment: ladders, pulleys, platforms, electric drills, scaffolds; devices enabling the craftsman to attack his chosen material at all angles and levels.

As Beatrice digested this, her ears were assaulted by rock music roaring from a pair of enormous speakers. Nothing mellowly funky, either. This was bang up-to-date, heavy metal or some such, more her brothers' style than her parents'. Cameron was clearly no dainty dabbler — he was the real McCoy. She grinned. The real McCameron.

Her grin faded as the real McCameron loomed on his threshold, a landowner confronting an intruder. Beatrice understood that no one, but no one, trespassed on this character's creative patch, and lived, or at least escaped without a burning earful. He dominated that doorway, guarding his domain, shielding even the sight of it from her.

She had been right about one thing: he was big. A hefty six foot plus, with a breadth of shoulder to match. Lean, lithe, but powerfully muscular. Beatrice had this passing whim that he had been carved out of the living rock, to ply his chosen craft. Or even, over the years, the craft had carved *him* out in the process? A fusion of man and medium?

His size wasn't all. He was powdered in fine dust from head to foot, including his denim overalls, but not enough to disguise his shock of red-gold hair, or his wiry beard, an arresting copper-bronze. He might come on, over the phone, like a Hemingway hero, but he struck Beatrice more as a tribal chieftain out of a novel by Sir Walter Scott. In his hand, instead of that chisel he was brandishing, she fantasised a bloodstained claymore.

"Beatrice Cole?" The deep drawl had to rise to a voluminous boom, in order to outdo his taste in background noise. She nodded. Her own vocal cords definitely weren't up to the competition. "So, you came!" His eyes were a rare blue, piercing, behind thick goggles: another disconcerting part of his working image.

Indignant, she opened her mouth to ask whether he'd doubted her intention of coming; then closed it, nodding again. "You're right," he confirmed. "I reckoned you wouldn't go through with it."

His smile was wide, lopsided, and alarmingly alive. It revealed a wealth of emotional conflicts and contradictions, as well as a full complement of white, slightly uneven teeth.

"So," he continued, "welcome to my workshop!" Only he was not making her welcome. He was blocking her way in, arms folded. Horatio, keeping the bridge; Hercules, facing the Hydra; Perseus, defying Medusa.

But Beatrice was no hideous mythological Gorgon. She was real, and sensitive, and returning his smile, deliberately cordial and relaxed.

Abruptly he turned and disappeared inside his lair. She could just see him, through the half-closed gap, as he strode about, switching off the cassette player and a few bright lamps.

Then he was out with her again, his voice preceding him through a sudden, stunning silence. "Come on! It's coffee time; I need my morning fix. We can sit over on the porch. Coming?"

He slammed the door, locked it, and set off across the grass towards his house. He had no need to glance back to see if Beatrice was following him. He knew she would be.

3

THE Cameron kitchen was not notable for its gleaming modernity; for that matter, nor was the rest of the Cameron household. But Mal did treasure his one indulgence: his electric coffee-maker.

When it came to most drugs — including alcohol and nicotine — Mal had always been scornful. In his opinion, no one should need to resort to artificial aids to heighten or deaden life's realities, whether creative or personal. Life was complex enough without approaching it in a glazed or dazed state. But he made an exception with coffee — and no one had ever suffered yet, as far as he knew, from passive caffeine consumption.

Abandoning Beatrice on the verandah, he dumped his grimy overalls among the heaps of garments on his bedroom floor, and went along to the bathroom, where he showered the stone-dust from his face, hair and body. Then he changed into clean Levis and crisp checked shirt, in her honour. When he reappeared on the porch, he was carrying two chunky beakers on a tray. He'd even located a cream-jug, and some milk to put in it: a miracle, considering he took his own coffee black.

The girl was sitting demurely on one of his well-worn cane chairs, gazing about with the bemused air of a displaced person, getting to grips with a foreign scene. Which, Mal reckoned, must be exactly how she felt, despite the superficial air of bravado.

He grinned to himself as he came through the French windows. One thing for sure, she'd taken on more than she'd realised, enlisting his help. But he'd bide his time, suss her out, hear the authorised version, as opposed to the true tale he suspected lurking behind it. Was she forgetting how well he used to know those Byrnes, back in the old days? He may have been no more than a mixed infant, compared to the adolescent Jim — but he hadn't been that young when he last saw Kerry. They'd both been, what, about the age this Beatrice was now?

And here was the point: no visually-acute person, such as himself, could fail to spot such a resemblance! It stood out miles: those intelligent grey eyes, the forceful chin, the defined cheekbones — a bone structure inspiring to any sculptor; the blonde hair, even worn like Kerry had worn hers, a cropped, sun-trapping cap. Yes, apart from Beatrice's strikingly dark brows and lashes, and a certain softness in her expression — a vulnerability which she clearly struggled to hide — the young Kerry Byrne could have stood there, in his workshop doorway, just now. Briefly, it had given Mal a real jolt; a kind of time-warp.

Oh yes, there was definitely a deeper connection here than she was choosing to divulge. But with what, precisely? With Jim himself? He always had looked a lot like his smallest sister — or vice versa. He'd last been back here to visit his parents before they'd all moved on, must be at least a decade ago. By the age of thirty-odd, he still hadn't been married. Mal wondered if he was now. He hadn't really seemed the marrying kind: became a brooding, introverted kind of adult, as if he nursed inner, unfulfilled yearnings.

Not that he hadn't been a real live wire as a young blade. Mal remembered Jim Byrne with a touch of recalled hero worship, as a charismatic youth in the late 'sixties; there were tales, probably apocryphal, of his exploits around the time of the Festival, in '69 . . . Of course, while Jim had been . . . sowing his wild oats, Mal himself had been a mere kid of eight or nine, barely aware of the events that had printed romantic Woodstock forever on the twentieth-century map.

The more he stared at this English

version of the Byrnes, this delightful Ms Cole — but surreptitiously, as he set the tray down on the slatted floor — the more vividly he was reminded of those days. How Mal and Kerry and their pals had spied on Jim's amorous adventures, whispering and giggling behind trees and doors! What a pain in the neck they must have been and how Mal had secretly envied the older boy's philanderings, elaborating them in his own fantasy world into sources of such searing excitement that they kept him awake nights . . .

Enough of such nostalgia! This was not the moment for self-indulgence, but for quiet watchfulness. He handed Beatrice one of the mugs, courteously proffering milk and sugar. She refused both; so much for foraging around for bowls and jugs in dusty cupboards. Then he sat in another wicker chair, which creaked as he made himself comfortable.

"Time I replaced these," he remarked. "The set used to belong to my parents, so it must have done twenty years hard."

"Have you lived here all your life? In Woodstock, I mean?" She was making prim small talk, but in this low cool voice, restrained, unshrill. And he did like the English accent, particularly in a female. Clipped; brisk — yet unaccountably mysterious.

"Sure. Born and raised here. Went to school here, like the Byrnes, only they got away." He studied her. "So, Beatrice Cole. What's your link with these Byrnes, then?"

He saw her flinch, though she concealed it well. "I've already explained," she said. "It's nothing really . . . just that I know someone who used to know them, and as I was coming here I promised to . . . "

"Used to know all of them, or only Jim?"

"Mainly Jim." She stared away from him, round his garden, then past him into his house. "At least, she never mentioned any others."

"So it was a she, this person who knew them?"

"Yes. Didn't I say?"

"You did not. Good friend of yours, is she?"

"We are — close, yes."

"Must be," Mal observed, "or you'd never go to all this trouble over such ancient history."

"Oh, it's no trouble! I wasn't doing anything else today!"

"And other days?" he said.

"Pardon?" Now she turned to face him. Those clear grey eyes; they could have been Kerry's!

"How are you spending your time, while you're here?" he said. "Is this some private adventure, a vacation, or what?"

Beatrice hesitated. "That's it, a holiday. I've been studying hard at University in England. Now I'm going to start a postgraduate course here. First, I decided to treat myself to this trip."

"Why here?"

"You mean, why the States?"

He shrugged. "If you like. Why this country, why this state, why this corner of this state?"

"Why not?" she countered, instantly.

"We get plenty of Europeans coming to pay their respects to Woodstock," Mal said. "But they tend to be a couple of decades older than you. I mean, it was back in the 'sixties, when the world and his woman made tracks to these parts, in search of new highs, spiritual enlightenment, art in nature, all that baloney."

"Of course I know that! My own . . . " Beatrice's mouth clamped shut; then, disarmingly, smiled. "Shouldn't it be 'the world and her man'?"

"We're into political correctness, are we?"

"We most certainly are."

"A touch outmoded, as a concept for the mid-'nineties, wouldn't you say?"

"I most certainly wouldn't," Beatrice retorted.

Mal heaved a sigh. "Don't tell

me you're one of these axe-grinding feminists? We have enough of those, this side of the Pond."

Again she fielded her smile — this unnerving blend, shyly radiant. "It's all right, Mal, you're safe. I left my cleaver at home."

"Whew!" He wiped his brow with the back of his hand, warmly returning her smile. She blushed deeply, which he appreciated. He could just be doing with this! This was forcing him out of himself, and it was far too long since he'd allowed anyone near enough to perform that tricky function. Inadvertently, this stranger, this outsider to the community, knowing nothing whatsoever about him, had wandered along and braved the challenge. If she only knew . . .

She was jabbering, perhaps covering her own embarrassment. "I'll be based in New York for at least a year. I'm looking forward to that."

"The Big Rotten Apple itself? It's one hell of a place," he said. "Has to be the most exciting, overwhelming city in the world, and I've seen a few. Found anywhere to live yet?"

"Not yet — but I'm used to London," she pointed out. "New York can't be much more overwhelming than that."

He had to admire her spirit. "Know anyone in New York? It always helps to have an ally, when you're let loose there for the first time."

"No." She bit her lip. "At least, I'm not sure . . . "

"How do you mean, not sure? Either you do or you don't!"

Beatrice sat bolt upright. This time she had gone pale, rather than pink. "I might know the answer to that," she stated, with considerable dignity, "when I leave here."

Mal was mentally kicking himself, for pushing her. He'd burrow to the root of all this, but he had to get his timing spot-on, or she'd back right off before he gave himself the chance. Play it cool, Cameron, he warned himself.

Keep your size elevens out of your big mouth.

He held both hands up, palms facing her. "I apologise. You're absolutely right, it's none of my business."

"I never said that," she protested.

"You didn't need to; it was written all over you. And I deserved it — I'm sorry. I have this habit of speaking and thinking, in that order." He leaned closer to her. "Listen, Beatrice. I go to the City quite often. I don't really enjoy it, I'm a country feller at heart, and I like to be where my work in progress is. But I do have to go, see my agent, take my stuff, organise it in galleries . . . "

"You exhibit in galleries in New York?"

Her interruption put Mal off his stroke. "Why wouldn't I exhibit there? I exhibit everywhere. New Jersey, New York, New England . . . and not just in the East. Not just in the States, for that matter.

She was colouring up again as she

realised her mistake. Not that it was her fault, misjudging the Cameron image. He deliberately affected this persona that was unglamorous to the point of scruffiness, but in his own field he was a force to be reckoned with. An acclaimed landmark on the international sculpture scene, his public work (though not his private life; he always kept them strictly separate) featured in Fine Art courses, catalogues, stylish magazines and glossy coffee table books.

He leaned back now, as far as the groaning chair would permit, stretching his long legs, folding his arms, dangling his empty cup by its handle from one index finger. "I've had a gratifyingly successful recent collection, which travelled through Canada last year, and is in several South American capitals this year. Next year, it's booked for Germany, France and Spain."

"I see — I didn't realise. I'm sorry, Mal."

"It's okay." Graciously, he forgave her. "I don't make a big scene about it, so why should you have known? I was only trying to say, I have to be in the City quite a lot, so I could help you out — show you what's what, where's where, maybe introduce you to a few contacts."

Beatrice was evidently taken aback by this new twist — as he had intended. "Thanks." But she soon recovered her poise: when she lifted her eyes to his, her cheeks had resumed their delicate rose, her voice its confident ring. "I really appreciate that. I'll have to see what happens . . . how things work out here. Meanwhile, if we could just . . . "

Before she could drag the subject back to the wretched Byrnes, Mal suddenly knew he wanted more time with her. He wasn't letting her grab the information she'd come for, sweetly smile her gratitude, then simply slip out of his consciousness as unobtrusively as she'd slipped in.

"Meanwhile," he cut in, "how do

you plan to spend the rest of your upstate break, before hitting town?"

"That depends," she said, cautiously.

"On what?"

"How long I stay, for a start."

"Well, let's put it this way. What have you done and seen so far? What would you like to see? What would you like to do?"

"I haven't had time to do anything much," she pointed out. "I only arrived two days ago. Also," she added, "this heat takes some getting used to. I came straight from an English summer, don't forget."

Mal seemed to be pondering, but actually he was thinking fast. "You like swimming, Beatrice?"

It had been a wise intuitive move. Her face lit up. "I love it."

"There are some great beaches round here, you know."

"But the sea's miles away!"

"We have fresh-water lakes. You must have heard about Wilson State Park, just down the road?"

"Well . . . " She looked faintly guilty: the tourist who has failed to do her homework and fears to offend the patriotic native. Which confirmed Mal's conviction that the lady was no tourist. If she was here for the sightseeing, he was a Cherokee.

"Did you bring your bathing gear with you?" he enquired.

"Yes, I thought there might be a swimming pool, but . . . "

"There's this other Park, bigger and better than Wilson, with one of the best views in the State. North Lake, they call it — up in Greene County, near Tannersville. You heard of that?"

Beatrice was looking distinctly uneasy. "I can't say I have."

"I could just use a swim, myself." Mal seemed to be staring into the middle distance, but he kept an eye on her all the time. "Months since I took one. How about us driving up there this afternoon?"

"What?"

He'd properly fazed her, at last. "I said, how about me driving you to North Lake this afternoon? It's been a long while since I got out anywhere, tore myself away from work, so you'd be doing me a favour."

"I heard you," she said. "But . . . "

"But what?"

"I don't think . . . "

"I'll bet you do think," Mal said. "I'll bet thinking's what you're best at in the world. Why not take a leaf from my book, for once; try acting on impulse first, thinking it through later?"

She was stiff and silent, as if he'd touched a nerve so intimate that it had temporarily paralysed her.

"Hey, Beatrice." He amazed himself by not only sounding, but actually feeling, gentle — even protective. "It's nothing so outrageous, is it? You don't have to come on like some Victorian dame that's been indecently propositioned? We gave up chaperones a long way back, in this neck of the woods. They went out with wolves and wampum."

She found her voice, but it was a bit husky. "I didn't mean that, Mal. I just thought . . . "

"That's what I'm saying. You do too much thinking."

"I thought you were so busy. I only expected to stay here a few minutes, long enough to pick up those addresses . . . I didn't mean to disrupt you, take up your time."

Disrupt him? Mal's eyes narrowed. He was well and truly disrupted now, whether she stayed around or whether she went. Might as well be disrupted for a ewe as a lamb. "Ah yes, we mustn't forget those addresses," he said. "But I don't believe you can't spare a few hours for a guided tour. Could be the best offer you get all week."

"I should imagine it's the only one I'll get," Beatrice commented.

"Well then. It's not one I make every day, either."

"I appreciate that, Ma . . . but haven't you got other . . . "

"Other what?"

He knew he was making it tough for her, but for some reason he was enjoying the way she was enmeshed in her own net — reluctant to admit her true motives for being here, or to share those burning questions which surely pressed from within. Mal was put in mind of the small fry, squirming on the end of those wire hooks they used to dangle in the creek as little lads. Maybe not so far from the time when whoever-it-was that Beatrice knew was dallying with Jimmy Byrne.

"Other commitments?" she was suggesting, carefully.

"Are we talking professional here, or personal?" he wondered.

"I . . . what about your family?"

"What family would this be?"

"I thought you might have . . . "

"I told you on the phone, Beatrice. I decide what I do, and when, and who with. Beg your pardon: with whom."

"And your wife?"

He scowled, but once again he had to respect her courage. Now she had reached the point, she came right out with it.

"My wife?"

"Wouldn't she mind — or would she come with us?"

"She'd have a job doing that." Mal's voice grated, so that Beatrice stared at him in consternation.

"Why? Where is she, Mal?"

"Where indeed? Who can answer that? Not me. She's not here, that's for sure." He stood up now, and began to pace the boards, hands thrust in pockets. But the girl didn't give up easily. Without warning, he wasn't sure how, he had lost his grip on this exchange — turned the tables back on himself.

"What's wrong, Mal? Where did your wife go? I know you're married, because you're wearing a ring . . . anyway, Solly said . . . "

So that was it! Typical woman, never

miss such a personal detail! And wait till he got hold of that darned motel-keeper, he'd . . . "Said what? What did Solly say?"

"Nothing, except he said 'they' when I asked him directions for your house. 'Their house', something like that. That's all."

"So naturally," Mal snarled, "you assume I'm half of a pigeon pair? Like all the rest, hey?"

"Not *all* the rest." She spoke calmly; her eyes followed his progress back and forth, back and forth; his rickety porch shook under his feet.

"Okay, not all. But with most couples, they fall out through choice. The romance fades, they get bored, they can't take the pressure. So they drift apart, maybe try all over again with Number Two, or Three, or Four. And where does it leave them? Where does it get them? Me, I believe in fighting through the hassles. That's what we believed, she and I."

He scarcely knew himself, could

hardly bear to hear himself, spilling all this pain out onto this unknown young woman. After so long, hugging the hurt to himself. Why now? Why her? Why?

"You and — your wife?"

"Correct. Renata. My woman — my spouse.

"Renata." It was agonising, yet extraordinarily comforting, the way Beatrice echoed the name, on a soft sigh.

All at once it was too much for Mal. He halted, directly in front of her, leaned down till his breath fanned her face, his nose almost jabbed hers. "You want to hear about Renata? You want the gory facts?"

"Only if you want me to know them." Her eyes were so close to his, they were a grey blur, asymmetrical, like a Picasso portrait.

"I want to tell you." He stood upright again, so that when he went on speaking, it was over her head, as if she wasn't there. She was the catalyst, allowing this to happen, but not really its target. Or was she? In any case, she said nothing, craning her slender neck to watch his face. He was subliminally aware of her expression, sombre but composed, as if she guessed what was coming.

"She was Austrian," he intoned. "Clever, beautiful, a professional potter, from Vienna. Well, from Vienna via Greenwich Village. We met at a crafts convention on the West coast one summer. She came back to Woodstock soon after, to visit me, and somehow she stayed on. We were together eight years — up until last Fall."

There was a long pause; then Beatrice murmured an encouraging "And?"

"And you know what? It would have been our fifth wedding anniversary, and her fortieth birthday, this month! Fourth July. I used to joke, lost my independence on Independence Day. Hah!" He glanced down at Beatrice. "Yes, that's right, she was a fair bit older than me. Nearly eleven years.

She was already well past thirty when we met, and I was a mere callow youth — about your age? That was why we never had kids, I guess — I was hardly more than one myself. Not that we wanted them; had our careers, each other . . . or that was the way we looked at it then. Now, I'm not so sure. At least something would've been left, if we'd . . . "

Mal subsided, leaning against the wooden wall, sweating, breathing heavily. His head was spinning, and again he was tormenting himself with *why*? Why pour out all this misery, today, when he'd kept it dammed up the best part of a year, this seething reservoir inside him?

Oh, there was plenty of local support, folk only too ready to offer consolation, or poke their noses in, more like. Renata had been popular. Spiky, unpredictable, like most creative types, but Woodstockians were used to creative types, and foreigners at that.

But he had held them at bay;

drowned his grief in this flood of work. Squashed it in stone, moulded it into one granite lump. Only in that form could he handle it.

Absorbing all this, Beatrice's demeanour had altered. Instead of that guarded severity she had shown so far, he saw perceptive sympathy. Whatever else his outburst had achieved, it had apparently dragged her out from behind her own laborious defences.

"What happened to her, Mal?"

"Died, last October. Car smash. Foggy night," he explained, gruffly. "Other guy was drunk, no lights."

"Oh no! Mal, I'm so sorry. So sorry!"

She was, too, he could tell; the way she leaped to her feet, and came over to him, hands outstretched in this spontaneous gesture of compassion. But she stopped short, a couple of steps away. She was British, after all, and she hardly knew him. She now knew this terrible, personal fact about him, but she hardly knew *him*.

"So was I sorry, believe me."

Her response had moved him, but calmed him, too. To his own astonishment, and surely hers, he smiled. The storm had passed very near, without properly breaking, but loosening the atmosphere around him.

Beatrice cleared her throat and stepped back. "I — I never realised," she said.

"How could you? Unless Solly said anything."

"Not a word. He might have wanted to; now I come to think of it, he did have a sort of look, as if he couldn't decide whether to let out some piece of juicy gossip, but I was in a hurry and I don't like gossip, so I never gave him the chance. I just took in how to find you, then left."

"Solly's the guy for wasting your time with tittle-tattle," Mal said.

"I gathered that. But it's not my thing, not at all."

"I can see it wouldn't be. Funny; it wasn't Renata's either."

"Unlike most women, you mean?" Beatrice said.

They exchanged slight smiles. Mal tried to fathom what was going on behind those unknown, yet oddly familiar, grey eyes. And what could she see, gazing into his? It was pretty damn peculiar, Mal thought, being presented with this reminder of days and faces long faded. Pre-Renata mostly, for goodness sake! And then, not being absolutely sure what Beatrice's real link with the Byrnes was. Ninety-five per cent sure . . . an educated guess . . .

She had retreated back to her chair, perched on the edge of it, still looking at him. He stood firm, feet planted apart.

"Okay," he said. "So now you've dug the dirt out of me . . . "

"It wasn't like that at all!" she replied, indignantly.

"I know — I'm sorry. I meant, now we've got that out of the way — how about my invitation? Would it be right and proper for you to accept, now you're fully briefed on my private life?"

Beatrice stared down at her hands, folded in her lap. "I didn't mean to intrude, Mal. I only came to . . . "

"We both know what you came for, Beatrice. Haven't you already found more than you came for?" Then he changed tack, and his tone lightened. "Listen, I know you're tempted! Cut the maidenly hesitation, and come, won't you? I could really use the break, and the company. Since Renata — well, I rarely leave this place unless I have to travel. I live like a recluse. It isn't healthy! Ask anyone."

Was he pushing her again — too far, too fast? And that word, 'maidenly': should he have used it? He hadn't planned to, but it was so obviously fitting, it seemed to slip out of its own accord. She was, he'd swear to it, exactly that. Maidenly. Highly aware, behind that controlled screen — sensitive, understanding, perhaps wise before her time — but innocent of passion. That was it: virginal. Not that Beatrice's emotional life was any of his affair. Any more than his recent bereavement had been any of hers.

He was watching her. It was all right: he had not blundered. She was smiling. "Thanks, I'd love to come to this lake with you," she said. "On one condition."

"What's that?" But he suspected what it might be. *Give me those addresses first.* He ransacked his brain to remember where he might have shoved his old address book. Back of a drawer somewhere? His paperwork had gone all to pot since . . . Renata had been a surprisingly methodical creature. Her half of their shared purpose-built workshop had been a model of order. Now Mal had spread his own dark tide of despair through both sections. So he could kid himself she was still around, just occasionally, lost in his work — could try, at least . . .

"On condition that we find some lunch first," Beatrice was saying. "You take me to a nice place, not too expensive, and I'll pay."

Crowning the coup, she was beaming at him, a generous grin which reached parts of him where other smiles had failed to reach for many months. Dormant parts, which he had considered dead, but which now stirred like a sluggish creature emerging from enforced hibernation.

He shivered. Someone walking on his grave? Or Renata, shifting in hers? Or something far less morbid, more simple and organic? Then he steadied himself, grinning back at her. "I won't argue," he said. "I wouldn't insult you by refusing. Sounds a fair deal to me."

"Good." Beatrice stood up and stretched. "Can I use your bathroom before we go?"

"Of course." He ushered her across the shabby disorder that camouflaged his spacious living room, down the hall and into the spare cloakroom. It was marginally less untidy than the bathroom; but as Beatrice locked the door behind her, Mal found himself wishing he'd bothered to clean the whole place up a few more times, or have someone else come in and do it, these past blank months.

4

IT was a relief, being a passenger for once. Beatrice was glad to leave her hired car outside Mal's house and hop up beside him in his rugged station waggon. He refused to say where they were heading, except that it wasn't far, and judging by the complaints her stomach was registering, that was just as well. In her anxiety to get moving this morning, she'd skipped breakfast, which was always a mistake.

She could just hear Judith's motherly tones: "Never start the day on an empty stomach — you'll regret it by mid-morning!" Then there was Simon, who never left for his office before engulfing his boiled egg, cooked exactly three-point-seven-five minutes, and three pieces of wholemeal toast, the third spread with coarse-cut Oxford marmalade.

Now, they were a pigeon pair; a typical parental pair — on the face of it, at least. Since a few weeks ago, of course, Beatrice knew better. In her head, she had always known appearances could be deceptive; now here she was, herself tangible proof of that ancient adage.

She gazed through the car window, blinking back a treacherous threat of tears. That intense interaction she'd just had with Mal — that sudden access to his own internal sufferings — must have opened her up, exposed her where she had thought she was sealed in. Now, at this safe distance, came another shock: this ripple of affection for Judith and Simon, mingling uncomfortably with her still-smarting resentment. So much to work out, to work through — especially here, of all places. Wasn't that why she had come to Woodstock, after all?

But at this moment, she was more concerned with where Mal might be taking them to eat. Somewhere simple and unpretentious, she suspected: the kind of place she'd have chosen for herself. She'd only known him — what? two hours? — but already there was this oddly familiar sensation; as if she could predict his reactions, as accurately as an old friend's.

Purely a result, she reminded herself, of the emotional scene they'd just found themselves sharing. Such a rapport wouldn't last. Initial impressions weren't often reliable. How could they be, when such long-established truths as who your real parents were could turn out to have been false — empty mirages — all along?

This time, however, her faith was justified. Twenty minutes later he watched from across a formica-topped table as she tucked into a meaty hamburger in its soft sesame roll. "Real food," he said. "The genuine ethnic article. Okay for you?"

"Great for me. Just what I was hoping for." She took a swig of iced water. "Anyone can read the glossy brochures and find the glossy restaurants. You need a local to find these little diners."

"And like I said, they don't come more local than me." He was chomping a steak, medium rare, with salad and French fries. Slicing it neatly into bite-sized chunks, then using his fork to shovel them in. There had been a brief confusion when she mentioned chips, which he interpreted as what she meant by crisps.

"You say tomarto and I say tomayto," he chanted.

"I had the same problem with soda, yesterday," she told him.

"Why? What do you call soda?"

"We call soda what you call seltzer."

"So what do you call what we call soda?"

"Depends what it's flavoured with. Lemonade, or whatever. Our soda's always plain. We usually have it as a mixer, like with whisky."

"Two nations divided by a single language, isn't that what they say?"

She caught his eye. His smile was particularly wide and warm, causing crinkles to fan out at his eyes, adding deep laughter lines to the more recent map of distress. And he had these dense, copper eyebrows, which virtually met in the middle, so that when he frowned they tangled themselves together, giving him a perplexed look.

For no very good reason, Beatrice found herself stupidly mesmerised by such trivia, and was forced to tear her gaze away from his face, concentrating hard on her lunch. Then he was chuckling, and she was glad to share his lightness of heart. She felt pretty cheerful, herself. The food was tasty, and outside the sun was shining; a stimulating blend of pleasure with apprehension.

She returned his smile. "What's your work like, Mal? Would I recognise your style, if I saw it?"

"Wow!" He drummed two fingers on the table top. "How do I answer that? What's it like? Well, how much do you know about sculpture?"

"Not a lot," she admitted. "I mean, is it abstract, or realistic? Big pieces, or small, or . . . "

"You mean, is it like Henry Moore? That's all most people know about stone-carvings: Henry Moore. Large figures with holes through the middle, looking like they could do with a square meal. Or sometimes," he added, "a round meal."

She could see this was not a fruitful avenue of discussion, but she persevered. "Okay then, what ideas do you base your work on? What do you use to — to plaster it together?"

"Heavy-y!" He stopped chewing, to stare at her. "Is my work plastered together? Do I have any ideas?"

"You must have!" she protested. "You must build it on something?"

Mal was deeply thoughtful now. "I build it on feelings."

"Only feelings? Not intellectual processes?"

"Just feelings; experiences. My

emotions are tied up in my work. I wouldn't know how to separate them, even if I wanted to."

She tried another tack. "How about principles? Beliefs?"

"Good grief, I don't know!" He shrugged. "I don't go for all that doctrinaire stuff. Peace and love, I guess — will that do you?" He leaned toward her, evidently more concerned with her questions than his own answers. "What's behind all this, Beatrice? What did you study at college, for goodness sake? Philosophy?"

"No, Psychology. I like to know what makes people tick."

"Ah!" He nodded. "Mental notes are being taken. Scientific curiosity: I might have guessed. Well, how about this for a — what was the word — principle: 'an eye for an eye leaves everyone blind'?"

"That'll do very well." Beatrice felt chastened. "I didn't mean to imply I wasn't interested in you, as a person . . . just . . . "

"That's okay," Mal said. "We all have different ways of being interested."

"I expect my mother might have heard of your work." Beatrice was keen to make amends. "She's the artist; she knows the art world."

"You don't say! What's her scene?"

"She paints. She sells her stuff, too." Beatrice was proud, telling him that. At the same time, it went against her better judgement; heaven knew where it might lead.

"That's great! And with four kids to bring up? A busy lady!"

Beatrice frowned. "I don't remember saying there were four of us?"

"In the car, on the way here — when I was droning on about my family. You said you were the oldest of four," Mal pointed out. "So, what about your father? Is he an artist too?"

"No. He's an architect."

"Now that's a fine job. I always kind of fancied it, myself. When I was at graduate school, I did think of diversifying into architecture." It was Mal's turn to show a technical curiosity. "Did he study art and design first, your dad, or go straight into University, or what?"

"He did study design. That was where he met my mother — at art college." Now she knew it had been foolish, allowing the focus to shift to her. She must snap the portcullis shut, before he could invade any further. She wasn't prepared for any more true confessions; not yet.

Mal must have picked up her unease, because he wasn't pressing the subject. "I'll get the check, shall I?"

"Do you mean the bill?"

They both laughed. "Another for our list," he said. "We should start a project — an Amer-English dictionary. Make our first million."

"It's bound to have been done before," said Beatrice.

Mal raised an arm and flicked his fingers, without turning his head. Immediately the waitress scurried towards them. He watched, impassive, as Beatrice produced a wad of dollars and clumsily counted them out.

In the car, speeding north, he had to swerve violently to avoid a graceful shape, dappled red-brown, which leaped out into the road just ahead. "Did you see that? Deer — dumb bastards! Suicidal maniacs! What's more, they wander into the garden without a by-your-leave and eat our zucchini. Or they did, when we used to grow zucchini."

"Was it really a deer?"

"You bet it was. Watch out for them, Beatrice, when you're in that hire-car of yours. Pretty creatures, but a hazard to life and limb. Ours too, remember — not only theirs. These roads are already death-traps, without them adding to the carnage," Mal said sadly.

She could only glance at him, finding no words to express her pity.

"Not many deer left in England, I heard," he went on. "But plenty up in Scotland. That's where my folks came from; did I tell you?"

"No, you didn't."

"My great-grandparents emigrated here, from up in the Highlands. It's in my blood, hills and high places. Ever been there?"

"No," she said, "but I'd like to. I've heard it's very beautiful."

"It is. I've been there, twice. I like to keep in touch with my roots. You'd never guess I was a Scot, would you?"

"To tell the truth, I did sort of suspect," Beatrice admitted.

"How come? Oh, my name, right?"

"Among other — attributes."

"What attributes? Kindly explain that cryptic remark, Ms Cole!" The tribal chieftain snarled, his red mane bristling, his strong hands grasping the nearest menacing object, which happened to be the steering wheel of one of the deadliest weapons devised by man.

"I can't really say," said Beatrice.

* * *

An hour later, she stood beside the leader of the clan McCameron, at the top of one of those high places that were close to his heart. He had promised the view would be stupendous, and it was.

"Fantastic!" she breathed. Her eyes were transfixed, behind her sunglasses; soaking it all up. The vast spread of it, so much rolling green country, so few marks of humanity; and the serpentine curves of the broad Hudson, slicing its path through the valley. It was spectacular. She must record it, imprint it, so that she could summon it at will from her store of perfect images. Also, so that she could relay it to Judith, who would want to know about everywhere she had been, everything she had seen . . .

"Well worth the sweat to get here, hey?" Mal was drawling.

It had been a slog, true enough, from the car park, through some woods, uphill at the height of a hot afternoon.

"It's wonderful, Mal! Thanks for

bringing me here."

"You're more than welcome; I told you, Beatrice, you're doing me the favour, donating your company. This is my first day out for far too long; I feel — I don't know — stir crazy, I guess! These wide open spaces, out here all the time, while I cooped myself up . . ."

"Gate fever." With an effort, Beatrice detached her gaze from the view and onto his profile. "It's not surprising you haven't wanted to go out, or mix with people, Mal. No one could blame you. But I'm glad if my being here has — I mean, if it's made you feel like . . ."

"It's made me feel like a number of things."

Mal, still staring ahead, moved a step sideways, so that the side of his body came into contact with hers. Beatrice gasped — prickling all over, as his heat mingled with her own. She looked sharply to the front; but she did not move away. This magnetism — this strange warmth they generated between them — was new to her; and yet she felt she had been waiting for it all her life. It couldn't be personal; it was just good old chemistry, surely? Love — the real thing, whatever that meant — couldn't happen all at once, in a matter of hours. Could it?

She had known sexual attraction; she was twenty-one years old, after all, and human. Mind you, at school and college, the boys around her own age had generally left her cool, if not cold. She had plenty of friends of both sexes, but failed to thrill when any of the male ones tried to approach more closely. Which had been convenient, since Beatrice had work to do, goals to achieve.

There had been that finalist in the English Department at University; if it had been up to him, matters might have developed beyond those tender, tentative kisses, which had certainly stirred her up — but only led to the realisation that some vital ingredient was missing, and although it might be pleasant, it wasn't worth the risk of involvement.

Budding psychologist as she was, Beatrice sometimes wondered *why* she had turned out so fastidious — so *sensible*! Now she was beginning to understand. Unlike most young people, who have to learn wisdom through maturity — unlike her own mother, for example — Beatrice was born sensible. In fact, standing up here beside Mal, oceans away from Judith, it occurred to her that she had often felt older than her mother; as if the infant Beatrice had become an instant adult, in order to compensate for Judith's insecurities and indiscretions.

Nothing would induce Beatrice to take any step, until she was certain the outcome would be safe and right. Up till now, at least. Today, she found her immunity slipping; found herself plugged into this universal grid, which she'd secretly feared she'd be denied access to forever. Human emotion: once its current caught you, there was no escape. She remembered how Judith had described the experience — as if you found yourself through another individual. It wasn't a question of loving, liking, or even knowing the person, she'd explained. You had to want them; to want this switch to be thrown by them; and that was enough.

At the time, Beatrice had pretended to understand, but actually it had been like listening to a foreign language. Here, so far away, in a rush of empathy with her mother, she did understand; she even forgave.

Beatrice didn't think she believed in fate. Judith did, but Judith was a natural romantic; Beatrice definitely wasn't. She recognised chance, surely not the same thing? Chance, and mutual need, had trapped herself and Mal together. Commonsense told her the more they struggled, the tighter they'd become entangled. Let the mysterious contact run its course, and they'd glide smoothly out, the richer for the encounter.

All the same, some risks she was not prepared to take. There might be a satisfying logic, a catharsis, in Beatrice recreating part of her mother's youthful story — the same age, even the same place; but there the echoes would end. Judith, flower-child of her generation, had cast every drop of caution to the winds. Beatrice, modern woman, must preserve a realistic sense of responsibility in the midst of adventure.

At first, on hearing the tale a month ago, Beatrice had blamed Judith. Not any more; how could she, when her own existence owed itself to that careless moment of passionate anonymity? But that had been of its era, her mother's era; her own era was now. The late 'sixties, the early 'nineties, only two decades apart, but it was hard to imagine more different times. Superficially, you could indulge in all the same actions, but underneath they had only the barest essentials in common.

While she was processing these

profound thoughts, Mal was speaking. No words percolated through the confusion in her mind, but his frame rumbled against hers as if it might convey the gist from skin cell to skin cell. He was also pointing, and she disciplined herself to listen.

"Over there," he was saying, "you can see right into Massachusetts. Those hills in the distance are the Berkshires. It's too hazy to see them properly today, but in winter they can be crystal clear. Then the Green Mountains, all the way to Vermont. Can you believe that, Beatrice — you can see three States from here? Doesn't it give you this incredible sense of power, seeing it laid out down there?" He raised both arms in a salute to the sky. "Hey, I feel good! I feel real, human, for the first time in months! This is a great thing you're doing for me, you know that?"

"I didn't provide the view," she said, not taking her own eyes off it.

"That's not what I mean." Now

he turned to take hold of both her hands, so that she had to face him. His hands were firm and enveloping; she was forced to crane her neck up, in order to see his face.

He must be ten inches taller than her, and so much stronger! *A real man*, her mind's voice taunted. An accident of nature, she lectured it — even as the rest of her was busy dissolving in a pool of instinct . . . no, more like a long-suppressed appetite, a sharp hunger, suddenly permitted to make its demands, complete with gnawing pangs and cravings.

Mal . . . male. The thing had its funny side, when for once she gave way, stopped agonising over it, working it out in her head . . .

"Regretting this, Beatrice?"

He had sensed her softening, then her moment of withdrawal. His hands tightened, and again she felt his voice as an extra physical dimension through her, almost within her. "What is there to regret?"

"Nothing — yet. Or maybe, that you followed your trail, to me?"

"My trail? Oh — no, I'm not regretting it. Of course not."

"That's good. Because you shouldn't."

Then he was bending down to her, his hands releasing hers, then sliding up to take her by the shoulders, astoundingly gentle considering the span, the force of those fingers. His face was close to hers, and closer, his beard tickled her cheek, her chin, her mouth. His lips were in amongst it, soft against her mouth. They seemed to be testing, tasting, teasing for an entry — or perhaps an answer.

Beatrice had questions of her own, huge elemental ones, an oppressive weight of them, all at once intolerable . . . she caught her breath, as her hands came up to clutch his hair. Her mouth trembled; the pressure of his sent further tremors right through her. Then she opened to him, inviting his intrusion, a promise of fusion . . .

But he drew back, quick and abrupt,

as if she had scorched him. She might be ready for this — but, after all, was *he*?

He seized her hand. "How about that swim, hey?" His voice was confident, but slightly hoarse. "Let's get back down to the lake."

"Okay." She felt ripped apart, abandoned — but she retained her dignity. Her breathing was still steadying to normal as she set off across the grass, a step behind him, almost running to keep up.

At last he dropped her hand, and slowed down. "I'll tell you something that'll interest you," he said. "There used to be this fancy hotel, right here. There's a board somewhere, with the details . . . it was all the rage, way back in the 'twenties, maybe even earlier. They had to ride a special cable car up here, because you couldn't reach it by road. You can see the remains of it, bits of old iron . . . the walls of the kitchen garden — see, over there?"

Following his pointing finger, Beatrice

could only nod. He was right, it did interest her, but she didn't yet trust herself to speak.

"Weird, isn't it?" he went on. "Here we stand, among all this grass, weeds, wild flowers — right where they had their ballrooms and banquets, chandeliers, wall-to-wall flunkies. Imagine the dramas that must have been played out, where we're standing; the flirtations, the scandals, the scenes . . . I always meant to come up here at night, see if I can trip over a time-loop. I'll bet this place is a regular flurry of spooks and spectres!"

Beatrice shook her head, smiling. Flesh and blood, the inexplicable responses they engendered, were one matter. Such whimsical fancies were quite another. "What happened to the hotel?" she asked.

He walked on, and again she hastened to keep up. "They burned it down. About when I was born — not far off thirty years ago."

"Who burned it down?"

"The owners, I think . . . I'm not sure."

"On purpose, you mean?"

"That's right. It became structurally unsafe, or something — I don't know, it always sounded pretty crazy to me. Patronised by presidents, jet-setters, all the fashionable people — you'd have thought they could rebuild it! But no, they condemned it. The whole giddy-scene, reduced to nothing but a pile of ash. Crazy."

He slowed his pace to match hers, offering her his arm, which she took. Eventually he asked: "You thinking what I'm thinking, Beatrice?"

"That depends on what you're thinking," she said.

"I was thinking about what I just told you."

"Then I might well be," she said.

"It sounds like a kind of symbol, you know? For our times?"

"Funnily enough," she said, "I was thinking something along those lines."

And funnily enough, it was true.

"This beautiful building, in its exotic setting — the music, the lights — the solidness of it, the colour, the form . . . "

"Like a magnificent sculpture," Beatrice pointed out.

"Right." His arm squeezed hers. "Then, whoosh, pow! The smoke and flames. Now, the silent, empty space."

After another pause, Beatrice said: "I suppose, if they destroyed it deliberately, no one was hurt?"

"We can only hope not. Apart from a few rabbits. Which is more than we can say for this beautiful planet, whether we idiot humans destroy it on purpose or by accident. Still," he added, "we should look on the bright side."

"Is there a bright side?" Beatrice hung back now, subdued. Suddenly she felt unbearably hot; stifled. The sun glared, and so did she. The ground sweated, and so did she.

"Sure there is! There's a cool, uncontaminated lake, just a few feet below us, slung up in these hills like a hammock — like a goddam miracle! We've lived long enough to see it, you and I, Beatrice, and in a few moments we're going to immerse our overheated bodies and soothe our jangled spirits in it."

He halted, facing her, and she gazed at him, marvelling at such quicksilver changes of mood.

"And I'll tell you another miracle." He grinned. "A man-made one this time. There's this flask full of ice in the trunk of my car. I loaded it from my icebox, while you were in my bathroom. Should be just turning itself nicely into ice-cold water by now. So let's get on down there, Ms Cole, before we both melt clean away."

5

MAL waded out into the lake, relishing the way the water silently parted for his hot, solid frame, then closed around it again. Whoever, he wondered, said that water had to be liquid? The lake seemed to him, as he struck out into it, like one dense sweep of green-grey marble. He slipped right under, leaving a seamless surface, Imagining no sign, not a ripple as he hung in there, toes touching the muddy bed, arms floating loose. Eyes, nose, mouth, lungs closed; all systems suspended. Life, for a few precious seconds, suspended.

It felt significant: a ritual cleansing. But of what? Sin? Grief?

He seemed to feel it rinsing ten months of accumulated limestone dust out of his hair and scalp, nails and skin, eyes, nose and ears. He felt scoured, much more than his daily showers could achieve. But was it penetrating deeper, to those grimy inner deposits? Sin was original; could never be washed away because it regenerated itself, part of our human make-up. But grief? Grief would always be with him, or so he assumed. It would develop through stages, as it already had.

When the tragedy happened, there had been blind shock. Then fury: violent torments of it, when he had locked himself in his workshop — their workshop — and hurled, hacked or pulverised everything he could lay hands or hammers on; until all traces of Renata were reduced to rubble.

Then this darkness had filled his head, so he was nothing but a black void with this mockery of flesh holding it together — forcing him to eat and drink, even though he knew he had disintegrated, along with those pots, tiles, lumps of clay and stone, models and maquettes.

After that, a frenzy of work. His

project, an obsession by day and by night these past weeks. His greatest piece yet; no eyes, apart from his, had as much as glimpsed it. When he started it, he had never intended it to be seen. He had intended to create, then immediately destroy, as real life did . . . but now, this bright day, he was not so sure. It would be finished soon, and he needed to decide, if only because it occupied one whole section of the workshop; the part that used to be hers, of course. What would she have said — Renata? What would she have advised him now, if she'd been there?

But he was being an idiot: if she'd been here, none of this would apply! He wasn't making sense, not even to himself. So how come he seemed to be making some kind of sense to this Beatrice, this English manifestation? Mal was no fool: it stood out a mile that she had drives of her own, internal ones, drawing her there — to him.

For a start, all that stuff about

the Byrnes: he'd get to the heart of that, given a bit more time. But her true motives were more complex. She needed something from him; but something obscure, or obvious? If so, why? Even more if so, what did he propose doing about it?

Which led him back to Renata. When he'd first seen Renata, all those years ago, he knew he had to have her — and keep on having her. The instant he'd touched her, he'd been hooked. Arrogant, twenty-one, he'd experimented his share, reckoned himself pretty worldly. But since then, never another. Renata had conditioned him, spoiled him for the rest. She had been his cosmos, his muse, his feminine apotheosis.

Not that Mal was so highly moral as to disapprove of playing the field; just that he'd had no urge, not the slightest temptation to glance elsewhere. Renata had absorbed him. She was so maturely rooted in herself, firm as a reef. In her arms, at her hands, Mal and his talent had flourished. She had enabled and fulfilled him. It had been enough, more than enough — and then, it was gone.

He might have tried obliterating his sorrow in other women's arms. God knew he'd had offers, though what warped pleasure *they* would have derived from it was anyone's guess. Mal never wanted to lay a finger on one of them, still less anything more.

But with Beatrice, he felt this shift, this welcome new movement. She knew nothing about him, which made a universe of difference. All she'd come searching for, when she came searching for him, was some old address, a slice of history. Now she'd found him and she clearly wanted more than that, which had to mean something — something about *him*, Mal Cameron, what he stood up in, what he had to offer. This knowledge refreshed him, like a dawn splash of cold water after a stifling nightmare.

Go ahead, Mal! Here's your chance

to wake up! You can give, and take, in equal measure; isn't that what we always said love was about?

Those were surely Renata's words! He could hear her voice, the guttural cadences of it, sharp in his mind for the first time in nearly ten months! But was he just making it say what he wanted to hear? Was he bending Renata's memory to his own will?

He considered it, and decided not. She was too strong for that, even in death; perhaps especially in death.

Mal turned over and floated on his back. "Okay Renata," he thought, since you're communicating with me: how do I resolve this other puzzle — this more personal connection, the one Beatrice knows nothing of? I'm not ignoring it but how do I confront it? I mean, he mused, "let's consider the facts. Beatrice has the look of a Byrne, right? It's not hard to speculate how this came about, but that's her business, she'll tell me when she's good and ready. *My* business is, she looks like Kerry did, nine, ten years ago, when I knew Kerry pretty well — before I knew you, Renata . . . so what's this? An attempt to recapture my lost youth?"

Naturally, Mal realised that any resemblance ended at the features. Beatrice neither sounded, nor acted like a Byrne. She was bright as a button, and so was Kerry, but there was American 1970s-bright and British 1990s-bright, and it seemed to Mal that they had little in common. Different times, different places, different ways.

Then Renata's voice rippled through the water to him again.

Hey pal, quit this soul-searching! You have a future, you're not all past! There's only one way you'll ever resolve this, and that's by trying it out — take the plunge! So, you run the risk of one or both of you getting hurt, but you know what I always said, Mal: the only trite failure is failure to try. If you don't try, you'll never know, right?

Mal jerked upright in the water,

rolled over on his front and struck out for the deep centre of the lake. "Renata, you don't change," he thought — and suddenly there was no anguish, only acceptance. "You always were spot-on, and you still are! It's okay," he added, mostly for his own benefit; "I do know you're dead, I'm not as crazy as I seem. Here in this lake I feel, for the first time, how dead you are, and I don't — no, how can I say I don't care? I'll always care! I'll always rage and weep and pound my loss into the unreceptive stone. But I acknowledge it as a fact. I loved you, but you're dead, so I can't have you any more. Me, I'm alive, with desires that can't plague or delight you any longer. I was beginning to wonder if they could ever plague and delight *me* again. As of today, I find that they can.

Reaching a deserted stretch, he closed his eyes, held his breath and submerged himself. Under here, there was just this enormous silence; and if a few final tears stained his cheeks, they would vanish into the hospitable depths of the lake, and no one need ever see them.

"Thanks, Renata," he thought, "for letting me consult you, and for your advice, and your absolution. And for eight memorable years. And for this lesson in immortality. I want you to know that while Cameron remains clothed in decaying humanity, *you* won't die."

Then his lungs had had all the emptiness they could take, and he was expelling the vacuum, coming up for air — and action.

He shook his head violently, showering the surface with drops. Out here, the sunshine glinted its dance on the lake. Did he say it was a slab of marble? He was wrong. It was a rolling fluid, sprayed and slashed by twisting skimming forms; a spectrum of colour and noise, shouting, plopping, sploshing. He was here among ordinary folk enjoying themselves; he was here to enjoy himself . . . it was time he discharged some pent-up energy. It was time to be on the move.

Mal headed back to the crowds, away from this deep core of the lake. It was a while since he had swum, but he felt comfortable — liberated, with his fast crawl. All things were possible to him, after all.

He saw Beatrice just as her voice cut through to him across the watery babble. "Hey, Mal! Wait for me!"

He waved. "Hi, Beatrice."

She swam to him, a steady graceful breaststroke. She had been right under, too, her sleek fair hair plastered down, darkened; and she was smiling. Had she, too, been working out her past and future with the help of the lake? Mal could see she was having a good time. He had brought her here, so it was due to him; he felt good about that.

"Hi!" he said again, as she slowed down, treading water beside him.

"Hallo." Now she was here, she seemed uncertain. She was tantalising, such an unusual mix of toughness and vulnerability — a conundrum in her own right.

"Great, isn't it?" He smiled back at her.

"Great! I love it!"

"You swim well," he said. "You've put in some practice, even if you don't get many chances back home?"

"We have plenty of public pools, but we can't often swim outside. If the air gets warm enough, the sea hardly ever does, and even then it's so polluted . . . "

Mal noticed she was looking tired. "Come on," he said, "let's go farther in, where you can stand."

But she was indignant. "I'm all right, honestly!"

"Okay then," he said. "Where *I* can stand."

Despite her protestations, he knew she was glad to follow him to where the lake sloped to a gentle shallow. He stopped when his feet touched the bottom and the water reached to his chest. He reckoned she should be able to stand there, keeping her head above the surface.

"You disappeared!" she accused him. "I looked for you everywhere. I thought you'd . . . "

"Drowned myself? No way, Beatrice. I've got a lot more living to do yet, before I kiss the world goodbye. No, I was taking a few quiet seconds underwater . . . best place I know for just being yourself."

"The thing is," she explained, "I'm shortsighted. When I swim, I have to take my contact lenses out, so I don't see very well — things tend to be a bit blurred. I was looking among the people for a bigger blur than most, and I sort of panicked when I couldn't spot you."

"I'm flattered to think you panicked when you thought you'd lost me. But believe me, Beatrice, I'm fine."

"That's okay then," she said.

"I hope I'm not blurred to you now?" He glided closer to her. She stayed still, swaying with the lake's motion.

"Oh no," she said. "You're crystal clear."

"That's great," he said, "because you're closer to me, too . . . I see you as clear as I've seen anyone for a long time; clear enough to know . . . "

"Know what, Mal?" Those lucid Irish-Byrne eyes stared right at him. They may not see so well, but they looked beautiful. He was delighted, at the way she didn't suffer from false shame — false coyness — as so many women did.

"To know I'd like to see a whole lot more of you." He reached out to take her by the shoulders, drawing her towards him. "Also, I'd like to *feel* you; feel more of you."

There was this tug of resistance, but it was only created by the lake. Beatrice slid into his arms without a twitch or a twitter of protest. Mal felt imbued with elemental force, a powerful magnet. She was a lightweight, anyway — but in the water of course she weighed nothing. Effortlessly, a lunar lover, he lifted her, so that her face came up level with his. She was silken soft, all over, making him feel rough and hirsute. Her limbs were smooth, lightly tanned, pale through the opaque water. Her blue one-piece swimsuit was smoothly clinging.

He set her down again so that he could explore its shape — her shape — with both his hands. Above the waterline, then below, then above again. She continued to stare up into his face, never pulling back.

Her shoulders, waist and hips had a proud curve, despite her slimness. Maturing, she would fill out, and Mal felt inspired by that knowledge. He made a note of it in his creative mental file; he might recall it, transpose it to permanent stone, one day. Each human form was special, unique. This was another way in which he held the gift of immortality.

Her body was warm, alive, gratifyingly

responsive to his touch. His logical brain reminded him how women's bodies behaved, immersed in water. A touch of chill, a touch of excitement, combine to activate certain physiological circuits, nothing personal, nothing intimate . . . but Mal chose to claim Beatrice's signals as his own. They added to his potency, his potential; it had been a long barren time, and he needed all the confidence he could muster. Today, by some magic, he could feel himself unfolding: his self — that inner man who had been tightly knotted up, locked in the dark; who had never thought to find or take this opportunity again. A shock to his system — but a positive one; the big question was, exactly what action to take? Mal had been emotionally and physically bottled up; now he must proceed carefully, let go gradually — for Beatrice's sake as much as his own.

But he could sense how pliant she was. More than acquiescent; cooperative. Firm, but so tender in his arms, nestling against him. He imagined that she felt safe there, in that public place, with so many other folk around. But safe from him, or from her own feelings?

She was new to this game, that was evident — precisely how new, Mal wasn't certain, but new enough to merit extra consideration. He'd give her every chance to backtrack, at every stage. The point of no return would be at her discretion, even more than his. He was prepared to carry full responsibility for his own actions — but not hers.

Still lifting her, his hands around her waist, he leaned in to kiss her. He wanted to, and he knew she wanted him to, so he took his step, this male initiative. Her skin tasted gloriously of fresh lake water, earthy. He'd been on the point of doing this, up there on the hilltop, but he'd shied off, not feeling prepared — braced. Now, he felt completely different; totally prepared, in every way.

Her lips were receiving his, parting, forming a statement and a question. He answered her question with his own statement. They sealed their pact, without restraint; the length of their bodies cleaving together, one double human shape in the enclosing, concealing water.

This was how it was done, Mal remembered that. And his body remembered, all too vividly. Yes, his body was leaping into life; against Beatrice's sweet mouth, he grinned an ironic pleasure in the living proof of being a man, and being alive. Then he drew away, set her gently down, pressed his lips to the top of her head: a promise, not a valediction. His pleasure deepened when she looked straight up into his eyes, with a smile as generous as his own.

"I think I'll go and get dry," she said.

"Fine. I'll just take another swim, if that's okay with you?"

"Of course it's okay. Take as many

as you want. See you when you're ready."

With a jaunty wave, Beatrice set off up the beach, leaving Mal to one final, vigorous private foray, back to those discreet depths at the centre of the lake.

6

BEATRICE had always loved this feeling: pleasantly tired, taut-skinned, late-afternoon, after an energetic swim. If it had been hot, you felt cool. If it had been cold, you felt warm. You felt stretched, invigorated, all over; surely the best exercise in the world, as well as the best relaxation.

And that was only the swimming! Add a few mysterious extra ingredients: a place like North Lake, a companion like Mal Cameron, and you had the perfect cocktail for an exotic summer evening.

In Mal's car, heading back to Woodstock, she shut her eyes and recalled every vivid minute of it. Already those minutes seemed out of time, unreal — and yet they had produced the most real, immediate responses she had ever known. She glanced at Mal: he was whistling to himself, keeping his eyes on the road, his hands on the wheel, his carved profile turned to her, and his mind on — who could tell what?

She gladly shared his silence, but inside her, this bubble was forming; this pearl of gratified surprise and delight. The first kiss, up on the hill, had been a kind of experiment; hardly more than a provocation, leaving her more bewildered than fulfilled. But the second one, the aquatic one, had been a revelation. She had been sorry, but not upset, when it had to stop. Later, when they were alone, they wouldn't have to draw back — not if she had understood Mal's intentions, and made her own plain.

Beatrice astonished herself most by not feeling guilty or nervous. She felt absolutely right. It was as if someone else — or perhaps another part of herself — had written this script, planned this interaction in advance, and all she had to do was play it out. She did acknowledge that she was using Mal, in a way, but wasn't it mutual? Wasn't his need just as acute, and even less personal than hers?

He had been widowed, nearly a year ago, after what was apparently a vibrantly happy marriage; since then he had been, in effect, a recluse — cutting himself off from basic human contact — until she had strolled along, insignificant visitor from England, inadvertently offering him this chance to break out and break open at last. Clearly, he was an intense man, a man with powerful emotional needs; and Beatrice had her own private blocks to shift — so if they were each bringing new life, new hope to the other, however it ended, could it be wrong?

Whose permission was she seeking, anyway, with all this soul-searching? No, it wasn't permission; she was merely confirming with herself. She did feel confident, but a spot of reassurance never did any harm. This was uncharted territory for her, after all. She knew there was no process simpler. She knew it was doing what came naturally. She knew all that, in her head. If she had been sixteen and drifting into her first adolescent fumble, she'd feel less self-conscious. At the ripe age of twenty-one, she was on the brink of old-maidhood — too old, compared with most of her friends, to be embarking on all this!

But Mal had almost certainly guessed the extent of her inexperience. Mal would surely treat her with care. What's more, he was right about something else. Mal read her, clear as a computer print-out: she thought too much and too hard. Her mind got in the way.

So, his explosive effect on her, at all levels, was not before time. And now it was happening to her at last, how did she feel?

It had felt wonderful, with Mal's body gliding, rasping on hers. The water lapping around the two of them, enclosing them — lending its own swirling caress, an alien element for a brand-new set of sensations. He was so broad and tall, where she was slight; hard, where she was soft, rough, where she was smooth. It emphasised his utter — how could she put it — *differentness*. What Judith would call his 'otherness'. He couldn't have been more 'other', in every way.

Beatrice admitted to herself how much she really liked and admired him. The way he had matured — lived, loved, suffered loss — retaining an acute sensitivity, beneath that calloused exterior. And physically, the way he was spare and muscular, not an ounce of flab — presumably from wielding all those massive mallets and things. He was easily strong enough to overpower her, if he chose. But she trusted him; she sensed he wouldn't choose. That was why she could afford to take this risk. After all, she had to trust some man, sometime.

She had only just met him, but she felt ridiculously safe in his hands — including here, in his car. He drove fast, aggressively even, but with a determined concentration. She imagined he'd tackle most challenges in this spirit: larger-than-life, but polished by control. Beatrice appreciated that; she wouldn't be able to cope with all this, if she felt that either of them would lose control for so much as a moment.

Now he was turning, smiling at her. Had she really only known him since this morning? Or yesterday evening, if you counted a slightly sticky telephone conversation? It seemed that life had shifted into top gear, speeded up like a fast-forwarded film — as if she had to cram new experiences into a short space, before the chance was gone.

It was only one patch of life, she told herself. Once this spurt had passed, it would settle into some kind of routine again. A new routine, not necessarily easy, but at a more normal pace.

He was saying something to her.

"North Lake all I promised?"

"More. You know it was, Mal."

He drove awhile, and then asked: "Are you feeling hungry?"

"I usually am," she said, "especially when I've been swimming." It was true, but it was another surprise. She'd expect to feel too much apprehension at a time like this; on the contrary, she was rumbling no less loudly than she had before lunch.

"Thought as much. My turn to invite you to dinner."

"Is it?"

"You can't refuse, not after I accepted your lunch-time hospitality so meekly."

"I wasn't going to refuse," she said. "I was going to say, thanks."

He nodded his approval. "Middle Eastern suit you?"

"Most food suits me. I have catholic tastes in tastes."

"There's a good place in town, serves all that stuff, you know, the hummus, the pitta, the falafels — Israeli, Greek,

Arab, Turkish . . ."

"You've persuaded me," she said. "But you'll have to excuse me before that, while I go back to the motel, to change and have a shower."

"You could take a shower at my place," Mal pointed out. "But I'll excuse you, because I have this proposition to put to you, and if you accept, I guess you'll need to collect a few bits and pieces."

Beatrice stiffened. What now? Was Mal about to take over, organise this whole event, rather than leaving it to chance or instinct? If so, in a way, she was glad. "Proposition?" she echoed.

"It'll get cool later," he said, "but not cold. Do you like sleeping out?"

She hoped he hadn't noticed her double-take. "Outdoors, you mean? In a tent?"

"I mean outdoors, but forget the tent. Who needs a canvas ceiling on nights like these? I mean, under the open sky. I do it a lot: it's beautiful, peaceful; a whole different world goes on out there, you know, Beatrice, from in the daytime."

"I can imagine." What Beatrice could imagine was wolves, bears, snakes, ghosts, escaped convicts . . . "No, I haven't done much of that sort of thing." She was trying to keep the quaver from her voice. "It's never really been my scene. But I'm game, if you're . . . "

"If I'm inviting you?"

Challenging me, more like, she thought. She was looking straight ahead, and his gaze was still fixed on the road, but she knew he was grinning.

"Are you inviting me?"

"Sure I am. Listen, I have waterproof rugs, quilts, inflatable pillows and padded groundsheets. I have flashlights, oil lamps, insect-repellant tapers. I have every darned gadget to make a lady cosy, and still find out how it feels to rest her weary bones on God's earth, with nothing between her and God's heaven. So, how about it, Beatrice?"

It was all very fine for him, waxing so lyrical and satirical. "Where would we go?" she prevaricated.

"I was thinking of this field, not far from Woodstock, known as Magic Meadow. Wonderful spot, bursting with excellent vibes. However," he continued, suspiciously solemn, "I reckoned that might not be such a great idea, because at this time of year we might not be the only ones. It's kind of, shall we say, renowned for nocturnal adventures."

"Adventures?"

"It'll be some adventure, if you never did it before," he said.

"Sleeping rough, you mean?"

"Whatever you prefer me to mean." He was grinning again. "Anyway, I told you, I wouldn't call it rough. Many a hovel will be more Spartan," he assured her, "than our nest beneath the Catskill moon. And whatever's new to you, Beatrice, that's an adventure, isn't that right?"

She had asked for all this, of course;

now she must rise to it. "It's a fine idea, Mal. I'd never have thought of it myself," she said, with profound accuracy, "but now you've described it, I can hardly wait."

"That's my girl."

"So, if not this Magic Meadow, then where . . . ?"

"How about right behind my house? My own neat field, the Cameron estate — at the edge of the woods, over the fence from the lawn?"

Beatrice smothered a sigh of relief. This struck her as the ultimate compromise. Hot-and-cold-running mod cons in the house, not too many yards away, somewhere to retreat to, if she was overcome with midnight trepidation, wondering whether the next rustle would be an owl, about to mistake her for a vole; or a disturbed porcupine, quills akimbo; or a buck, spiky antlers lowered . . .

But this way, it might be rather conducive. Romantic even — if romance was what Beatrice was after, which of course it wasn't. She took a down-to-earth attitude to this affair, as she did to most of life; and down to earth was certainly where they looked like being tonight.

"I like it, Mal. Thanks; I accept. So, what do I need to fetch — to wear, I mean?"

"Oh, leave the flimsy negligée behind. Bring your warmest sweater, sweatshirt . . . socks . . . if you haven't brought any with you, leave it to me. I have a wardrobe full. Some of it might be Renata's, but you wouldn't mind that, would you?"

Beatrice cringed. But was this new challenge aimed at her — or at Mal himself? He would have to talk about Renata openly, if this process they had started between them was going to keep rolling; she could see that, even if she didn't exactly like it.

"No, Mal," she replied. "I wouldn't mind, if *you* wouldn't."

Without her noticing it, they had arrived back at his drive. They had approached from the other direction, so it had crept up on her. One wooded steep winding road looked much like another, when you were not responsible for finding the way. He swung the waggon off the hill and up to the house. Her car waited dutifully where she had left it, as mindless machines have a habit of doing.

After he switched the engine off, they sat in a pool of silence, punctuated only by the twitters and chirrups of birds. The two of them seemed frozen; a statue, pinned in time. Was it that neither of them wanted to make the next move?

The last move out of one situation, Beatrice reflected, is the first move into the next. And in this case, the next would be as formidable as this would be straightforward.

Finally, Mal said: "This is how I see it. You go back to the motel now, get yourself ready, and in an hour or so I drive down, pick you up and we go on and eat. Then we come back here, and take it from there."

Take it from there. The phrase hung, almost visible, on the air between them.

"Sounds fine to me, Mal," she said lightly.

"Right." But he still did not move. When he spoke again, his tone had altered — gruffer, yet softer. "Beatrice, don't be offended — I have to ask you this. I have to make sure things go off well for us both, tonight."

She cleared her throat. "What's that, Mal?"

"It's not easy. I haven't done much of this, or not for a long long time. I want you to know, I've been with the same, faithful woman, most of my twenties — since then no woman at all . . . haven't even wanted to — till now."

"I see," she managed to whisper.

"And you, Beatrice — this is your first time, right?"

Before she could react, he had turned to face her; and he was so sombre, she was flooded with a sudden sour terror.

Was he about to reject her, abandon the whole venture, because she was fresh and unsullied? Was he about to balk at the sheer responsibility?

He was staring into her eyes; then he was speaking, fast, low, earnestly. With churning heart, she tuned in to his words.

"Yes, I reckoned I was right about that. Look, it's fine by me, Beatrice, if this is what you want. I think we understand each other. No strings, hey? You have your motivations, I have mine. I like you a lot, and I respect you all the more for your sincerity."

Beatrice was fielding this crashing conflict: relief, spiked with a new agitation. Breathing deeply, she muttered, "It's okay, Mal, I do understand — all of that, of course.

He was still examining her, so intently that she felt herself blushing. "Sorry to seem so unromantic," he said.

"No, don't apologise. You're right, we should — make these things clear . . . " But she dropped her gaze, obscurely ashamed at letting him do this vital spadework, when she was the one who was supposed to be so pragmatic, so upfront. Then she rallied. "It's just that I wasn't expecting all this, any more than you were," she pointed out, with as much dignity as she could cobble together.

He nodded. "I won't ask, why me?" he said, "or why now? None of that's any of my business. But we do have to be realistic, however we feel at heart. The free, devil-take-'em 'sixties are dead and gone. This is the strait-laced, look-before-we-leap 'nineties. We have to share this decision — look before we leap together, hey?"

Her eyes widened. He was even nearer her wavelength than he could possibly have guessed. But she only said: "You're quite right, Mal, and of course I don't mind. I did intend to share all the responsibility, and I'm grateful to you for helping . . . if I was a bit, well, stiff, put it down to . . . "

"Lack of *savoire-faire*?" he teased, but kindly.

"I was going to say, being in a foreign country," she retorted.

He leaned towards her now, conspiratorial. "Just one more point: go easy on me, huh? I'm out of practice — probably past my prime."

"Poor old man! We'll have the wheelchair parked ready, shall we?"

She was astonished at her own boldness, but she knew that laughter was the best tension-breaker.

Obligingly, he chuckled. "You're great, Beatrice, you know that? I'll tell you something. I'm looking forward to this evening, more than I've looked forward to any date in years." He paused, then went on, "Much, much more than I've looked forward to any damned thing, these past ten months."

"That's good," she said. "Me too."

He stared at her a few moments longer. She returned his stare now, level, equal — feeling curiously adult, sedate, as if she had come through a major test, and it was all over bar the shouting, when actually it had barely begun.

"Right then!" He charged into action, flinging his door wide, striding round to open hers. Crossing his drive, she found her gaze drawn — across the lawn, past his workshop, over the fence, into the small field, on the edge of the woods . . .

Over there. Tonight. An agreed, scheduled event, destined to happen, out here. Not just *in* the night, but in the night. No prying neighbours, but a skyful of winking, knowing stars. On the dank creepy-crawly ground, open to the wild mosquito-haunted air.

And why not? She had come to America in search of new discoveries, explanations. She might as well steep herself in new experiences, since she had apparently started this inexorable process.

Mal caught up with her as she reached her car. He smiled and took her hand. At the touch of his palm on hers, his fingers twining among hers, her insides clenched and tingled.

Neither of them spoke again, but Beatrice's mind was calling to him as she drove off.

Yes, Mal; I'm quite looking forward to this evening, too. And to this night. I think.

7

BEATRICE sat up to watch the sun rising over the folded hills, out through the clustered trees. First, searching pink fingers, then gold rays, then the orange rim. It would be another fine day. In two hours the temperature would start to soar, banishing this film of dew from air and earth. In four hours it would be hot; in eight hours it would be stifling. Now, it was pleasantly cool, but in the deep night it had grown chilly, so that she had been glad of her cotton tracksuit and a pair of Mal's hefty wool socks. And there was no need to emerge yet, not till necessity plucked her from this cosily macho cocoon.

Beatrice smiled, appreciating the contradiction: cosily macho. But it was apt; this sleeping bag was so snugly quilted, yet so belligerently khaki. Producing it, late last evening, from his loft, Mal had drawn her attention to its military origin. It was actually two heavy bags zipped together, with waterproof bases, all in that dour dark green.

"These guys," Mal had remarked casually, "were in Vietnam."

"Vietnam!" Beatrice had stopped in her tracks, half-way to his kitchen, arms full of inflatable mattress and pillows. "Are you, I mean were you old enough to be drafted? Surely not?"

"Lord, no. Work it out; the ceasefire took effect in '73, at which time I was barely into my teens."

"I can never remember important dates like that," Beatrice confessed.

"Ancient history. Defunct and buried." Beatrice waited, tensely clutching her bundle, there in Mal's hallway. She hadn't yet seen his frown so deep or daunting. "Not all of my family got so lucky," he finally growled.

"Some were drafted?"

"They were."

Yes, Beatrice sensed this whole new subcurrent of bitterness here. You could think you knew someone, in a short time, when all you really knew was superficial — intuitive. "What happened, Mal?"

"It was my two oldest brothers, went to 'Nam. One came back, the other didn't. And the one that did was never the same afterwards."

"Tell me," she urged. Of course, she had read and heard about this tragedy, seen films and TV documentaries — but only happening to someone else, long ago, far away. Except, she now understood, it happened to real people, like Mal and his family.

"You want to hear?"

"If you want to tell me," she said, putting her bundle down.

He shrugged, as if to indicate that the past could no longer hurt him; but Beatrice knew better: such scars would always be there.

"Shaun was caught by a 'Cong

sniper in some jungle hellhole. He never walked straight again, but at least he lived to get home to his young wife. She stood by him, all credit to her."

"I'm sorry, Mal . . . "

"Then there was Drew — the oldest. His plane was shot down while he was on some reconnaissance trip. Blew up, right under him." Mal shuddered, and Beatrice felt a wave of sick sympathy.

"I'm so sorry, Mal; I'd never have asked, if I'd known!"

"Why not? It's simple fact! You learn to live with it, like everything else life throws in your face. One blessing, though — at least Mother wasn't around to see it. She died when I was a kid."

Beatrice leaned on the wall. No wonder Mal was so volatile! The wonder was, how kind, calm, tender he could still be. And yet, perhaps, that was just what you might expect, from a sensitive person — especially a highly creative one — who has taken a battering from life. She felt uncomfortable, ashamed of her own self-pity. And she'd thought *she* had problems! "You haven't had it easy, have you?" she ventured.

Again the shrug. "What's easy? Shrinks might tell me I gravitated to a woman so much older than me because I lost my mother. Who knows?"

"You don't share the current craze for analysis and therapy?"

"I have my own way to work out problems," he said. "I don't grudge anyone else theirs. Mine's cheaper, and it does the job."

She was intrigued. "What's that?" She waited a long time for a reply, and when none came, she added: "You don't have to tell me."

He stared at her, or perhaps through her. He put the sleeping bags down on the floor, and leaned on the opposite wall, arms folded. At last he said: "That's true, I don't." Then he bent down, picked up the sleeping bags, and strode into the kitchen and out through the back door.

Beatrice preferred unsatisfied curiosity to terse hostility, so she had simply followed him. Outside his house, he had visibly relaxed, halted, dropped his burden again and turned to relieve her of hers. Then, disconcertingly, he had gathered her into his arms.

"I'm sorry, Beatrice." Now he was holding her tight, muttering against her hair, so that his words filled her head, intimate as her own thoughts. "I should never have brought that subject up. You were great, not telling me to shut the hell up, even at a time like this . . . "

"No, but Mal," she had tried to protest, "I didn't mind!" But her own voice was lost, muffled in his heavy sweater.

"Especially after such a great evening," he went on. "I apologise."

She had freed herself, smiling up at him, pink and tousled from the contact. "There's really no need, but I accept, if it makes you feel better. And it was a great evening, Mal. A delicious meal. Thanks."

He had returned her smile with his own — so wide, slow, sweet. "Come on then, woman! If we don't stake our territorial claim, the grizzly bears will get to our patch first." Then he had tucked the sleeping bags and everything else under one arm, leaving the other free to put round Beatrice, as they walked across the lawn through a dense dusk.

And here she was, this morning, still close beside him. Cosily macho — that phrase fitted the man himself rather well, too. More of the cosy, at this precise moment, sprawled next to her, his breathing remarkably gentle for such a big man.

Which also summed him up exactly, she mused, as a glow suffused her even at the words . . . remarkably gentle, for such a big man . . .

His macho side had been revealed a few hours earlier, balanced by a streak of protective chivalry. Beatrice was no expert, but she suspected, from the evidence so far, that he wasn't as rusty as he'd pretended to fear. Whatever obscure emotions motivated him, he was powerful — potent; that was probably the word.

Despite that, and the unexpected violence of her own new passions, she had no call for regrets this morning. This glow was one of gratitude; she felt cherished, uplifted, recalling the man's restraint. Mal had waited, watching her, holding back, always giving more than he took, until she had cried out her private pleasure into the dark friendly night. Later — still fully clothed, awakened yet uninvaded — she had wept in his arms: not tears of shame or loss, but a pure expression of feeling, a release. She felt happy this morning, because it had been not only delightfully innocent; it had been fun. They had laughed, whispering ridiculous communications — profound meaningless messages which they had both, as if sharing an instinctive language, understood.

She did just wonder, in the cold light of day, whether Mal had really enjoyed it as much as he had seemed to; or whether he felt deprived . . . she stretched luxuriously, gazing at the rising sun. An event she rarely witnessed, not being an early bird by nature. Open-air-fiends among her acquaintance droned on about this being the best part of the day, and she had to admit, they had a point.

Talking of birds, the feathered ones were starting up now, clearing their chirpy throats for action. Species swooped and flitted in these branches which British ornithologists would surely drool over, if they got a chance to fix their beady binoculars on them. Her parents, for instance — or rather, Judith and Simon — were interested in bird-watching. Mal had told her some names, which she had tried to remember for Judith's sake: gaudy native specimens, such as Blue Jays, Red Cardinals, Striped Sparrows. Beatrice had never spared much enthusiasm for this line of nature study, but out here she felt part of the animal kingdom. Mal had been right: it was a whole different world.

Yesterday evening they'd returned to a display of fantastic fireflies, sparking through the twilight. Then, in the night, so many sounds: calls and croaks, frogs and crickets, mysterious squeals and rustles which had sent her nestling closer against Mal's warm secure frame.

She had to concede that evidence of bears had been thin. The nearest contender might have been Mal himself: the way he'd enveloped her and reared over her, growled as he wrapped her in those strong rough arms, so that she'd known there was no escape, even if she'd wanted to.

He had displayed this delicately subtle balance of tenderness with fire, and the result was stunning — had literally stunned her feelings into new shapes, so that loose ends had fused together, tightened, and formed into one overwhelming emotion, one awareness.

She looked down at Mal's sleeping face. She was in love with him. Simple as that. She'd never slept in the open before, or slept with a man before, or been made love to before, or been in love before. Last night had been a quadruple milestone on her road through life.

As if feeling the pressure of her gaze, Mal grunted, stirred and rolled over. Then he opened his eyes, extricated his arms from the padded depths, and held them out to Beatrice. Without a word she lay down, moving into them. For several minutes she relished this new sensation: peaceful closeness, with her face buried in his neck, her body pressed to his.

Eventually, with suffocation threatening, she squirmed free and propped herself on one elbow. His eyes, staring up at her, were a deep sharp blue. "Hi,

Beatrice. Did you get some sleep?"

"Good morning, Mal. Of course I did — lots!"

"And how do you feel this morning?"

"I feel fine," she told him.

"Me too. You felt fine to me, too," he added, gruffly, "last night."

"Did I? Really?" He seemed sincere, and she blushed.

"Do you really need to ask?" he asked.

She trailed a fingertip down his brow, nose, chin, through the rich beard. "Do you need to ask how I feel? Can't you tell?"

"I told you yesterday evening, I'm insecure. Out of practice."

"I'd never have guessed," she said, boldly.

"Madam, you're too kind!"

She giggled, then frowned. "Are you sure it wasn't — I mean, you weren't — I mean, because we didn't . . . "

"Listen, Beatrice." His voice rasped with emphasis. "It was exactly, I mean exactly the way I wanted it. No more, no less. Believe me, thanks to you I feel — freed; refreshed; humanised."

"Good." And suddenly she felt full of life and a new energy. "Should we get up? You'll want to be getting on with some work . . . "

"Hey!" He grabbed hold of her, heaving her down alongside him. "Where's the fire? Gone off me, now you see me in daylight, or what?"

"Nothing like that; I just feel guilty at taking up so much of your time, when I know how much you have to do . . . "

"You have to be kidding, Beatrice! How can any person feel *guilty*, for goodness sake, when they just shared what we shared?"

"Easily," she said sadly, "when that person's female. It's programmed into our system; guilt is our middle name. You'd never believe how guilt haunts us, whether there's any need for it or not."

"Well, there's no need for all that baloney now," Mal snarled.

"All right, you've made your point," she said. "I'm sorry."

"That's better." He was studying her, as she lay beside him, now slightly subdued. "Would I be right," he said, more gently, "in guessing you have something on your mind, something to do with the reason you came here, which you haven't told me?"

It was so unexpectedly perceptive, she clenched inside, but her face registered only a cool stare. "That would be telling."

"And you aren't telling?" She shook her head. "Maybe one day, when we know each other better?"

"Maybe," she muttered, wondering why she felt it would be even more difficult to tell him the truth now, after everything that had happened, than it would have been yesterday morning, when she'd barely met him.

"Hey, don't go all droopy on me, Ms Cole! Not after such a gutsy performance this far. I never had you down as the droopy type."

“Isn’t everyone entitled to their moments of anxiety?” she countered.

“Morning-after angst?” he suggested.

“If you like.”

“Not really justified in this case, but we’ll allow you a special dispensation, seeing as you’re a novice,” he said, kindly.

“Thanks,” she said.

“Anyway, all this talk of getting up and getting out,” he pressed. “You wouldn’t think of slinking away, not till I find those addresses you came for, now would you?”

“I can have them, can I? You’re sure I’ve earned them?”

“Earned them?” Mal echoed. “Is that how it is? Wow, you must want them one heck of a lot, for this — how did it go? — this friend of yours, if you thought you were prepared to . . . ”

“It isn’t like that at all, as well you know,” she protested. “I’d forgotten all about them!” The amazing part was, she genuinely had.

“Sure, sure, I know. Only joking. But

listen, before I give you what you really came here for, and you disappear over the horizon . . . ”

“Mal! Do you think I’d do such a thing?”

“How do I know what you might do? I might know you pretty well, in one way, but I don’t know much about you, and perhaps I never will. Remember what we said? No strings, no complications?”

Beatrice was appalled at the way her heart sank. Such glib phrases: she supposed she had meant it, when she’d endorsed them last night, but now . . . now, did he really mean them himself? “I remember,” she said.

“So, please listen, will you? I have something important to say.”

“I’m listening.” She wriggled free so that she could see him. She needed to regain control over this situation. There was a new edge, something faintly threatening, to his tone.

“I have to tell you,” he was saying. “I should have told you before, but I couldn't. Now, I can't put it off any longer."

"Is it something to do with Renata?"

"No, this goes back way before Renata."

"What, then?" All that languid sensuality had drained away, so that she was tense all over. She had failed to be entirely straight with Mal, so far; now it seemed the game of charades had been two-sided.

"It's about your friends and mine, the Byrnes."

"Oh?"

"You came looking for Jim Byrne. Your motives are your own, but . . . "

"But what, Mal?"

"Quit squeaking, woman, and listen!" Mal wasn't finding this easy. "Presumably," he went on, "you never actually met any Byrnes?"

"No, of course not."

"How about seeing any old photos?"

"Why should I? I told you, they . . . "

"Yes, you told me, your only connection is this unspecified female friend, who knew the family years ago."

"Quite."

"What I'm attempting to tell you," he said, "is this. *You look just like a Byrne, yourself!*"

"Ah!" There was this dawning comprehension; very little surprise.

"Ah!" he echoed, as if her reaction had only served to confirm his own suspicions. "If you don't have Byrne blood running through those delicate blue veins of yours, I'm a . . . well, I just know you have. You're related to them, aren't you, Beatrice? I never saw such a resemblance. It's spooky — the eyes, mouth, colouring . . . "

"Oh God!" Beatrice slumped back on the air-pillow. Mal had loosened his grip on her, but not his gaze. This was a development she simply had not considered, fool, stupid fool that she was!

And yet, if it was so glaringly obvious, why had Judith neglected to mention it, recounting the story a few weeks back? Or had the finer details of Jim's features swirled away into some misty dream, leaving no more than a bleached bronzed vague youthful male fantasy?

Beatrice's mind churned Mal's revelation over: first one emotion, now another, like garments chasing each other round a washing-machine. She'd have strong words with her mother about this! Admittedly, she had never taken after Judith, physically. Her mother was dark, stockily built. Simon was fairer, slimmer, but Beatrice had never particularly resembled him either — though family friends and relations had often (ironically, as it turned out) claimed to notice a likeness.

No, but this notion that the Byrne genes might be so dominant in her, that she might strike Mal as a walking, breathing Byrne . . . it was surreal, outlandish, when Jim's role in her existence had been so brief; in a strange way, so impersonal.

It was perfectly straightforward, of course. His role had been precisely fifty per cent, no more, no less. It was the biological law, and it never varied. Beatrice was the product of his allocation of DNA, equally with Judith's, and superficially, by sheer chance, she had ended up with a greater share of his. The rest of her character could be attributed to environment, but as far as public display was concerned, heredity had caught her out.

Mal was watching her changing expressions. "You didn't think?"

"That I looked like them? It never occurred to me."

"But you do know why?" he persisted, very gently.

"Oh yes. Yes, I know why."

"So do I, I guess."

"I expect you can guess," she said.

"Jim? The link is Jim?"

She nodded. Head cast down, she murmured, "Jim, and my mother."

But Mal lifted her chin, one finger beneath it. "It's no big deal to me, Beatrice. Jim was a rare one for the girls."

"Is that supposed to be a comfort?" she snapped.

There was a pause, and then he said, "Renata used to say, there's this pattern in everything. Everything in life is connected to every other thing; every person to every other person. The sooner the world understands that, she used to say, the better world it will be."

"Clever woman." Beatrice sighed. "So, you guessed my connection with the Byrnes, long before I decided to tell you?"

"Almost the moment I saw you," he confessed.

"And you said nothing?"

"Neither did you," he reminded her. "I reckoned it was for you to keep your secret until it was time to give it up."

"And now it's time," she said.

After another pause, he asked: "Do you want to tell me the story?"

"About how it happened, you mean?"

"I can work some of it out, from your age, and the odd hint . . ."

"Can you?" Beatrice worked it out too. "Yes, I suppose you might."

"Your mother was British, not American?"

"She's English. She was an art student in London in the 'sixties and so was my father . . . or rather, her husband, Simon . . . "

Beatrice's voice trembled. This point had troubled her, ever since Judith had broken the devastating news. How could she call Simon her father, after learning that he wasn't — and yet how could she call him anything else, after so many years of relating to him in that way?

Mal was following her so closely, he might have climbed inside her head. "He may not be your father, genetically speaking, Beatrice, but surely the man who raises you, takes care of you, influences your ideas, attitudes, fortunes and all that — the man who calls himself Dad — surely he still has a right to be called your father?"

"You think so?" Mal's probe was so

accurate, she could only whisper.

"Don't you think so?" He frowned. "When did you find this out?"

"A few weeks ago — when they heard I was planning to come over here, to study . . . they decided they had to tell me, in case I . . . you know . . . "

"In case what? Like the plot of some blockbuster, you met and fell in love with your own brother?"

"Something like that, I suppose."

"You didn't plan to visit the States because you discovered this?"

"Not at all . . . at least, it was like some — compulsion. I always knew I wanted to come over here, so as soon as I got the chance, I fixed it."

"Hmm." Mal nodded. "You were about to tell me how it happened."

"I don't know much, really. Apparently my mother was sort of involved with Simon at college, on and off, you know; they didn't commit themselves but they were close friends, all through art school . . . then it was

1969, and my mother wanted to go to Woodstock . . . ”

“The Festival?”

“Right, the Festival. It was like a Mecca for her; she loved that music, and the whole hippy scene — still does, under the middle-aged exterior. She couldn’t persuade Simon to join her, so she got an evening job, saved up enough to take herself over there — over here.”

“Alone?”

“With a couple of fellow-students, I think.”

“And she was — what? Twenty?”

“About that, yes.”

“And at the Festival, she met this delectable local lad, Jim Byrne?”

“I suppose so, yes.”

“And had herself a romantic trans-atlantic episode with him?”

“A quick fling. Hardly more than a . . . ”

“One night stand?” Mal supplied, as she faltered.

“They slept out,” Beatrice explained,

"under the stars, together."

"No!" Mal chortled. "I knew I was challenging you, suggesting we spend the night out here — but I sure couldn't guess just how much!"

"No. They were on — Overlook Mountain, would that be right?"

"It would. So, you were conceived on Overlook?" Mal whistled. "Now, that is romantic, if you like."

"Is Jim — was Jim really — how did you put it — delectable, Mal?"

"Plenty of women thought so, let me tell you. We kids used to wonder how he did it. Like I said, your ma wouldn't have been his only conquest around that time, not by a long way."

"And like I said, that's supposed to make me feel better?"

"Why should you feel bad? It's not your fault; and Jim Byrne's a great guy — smart, handsome — you could do worse than have him for a pa."

"I'll have to take your word for that," she said.

Mal waited a moment, then asked,

"What happened after your mother got home, Beatrice? Did she tell your father — Simon, that is — or what?"

"They got together again, almost as soon as she was back. The separation made them realise they were in love with each other. When she found she was pregnant, she told him, and also told him it couldn't be his. Appearances mattered more in those days than they might now, so he said they should get married at once, and he didn't mind about the baby, as long as they never told anyone else."

"Not even — the baby itself? Not even you?"

"Not even me. And they never did — until a few weeks ago."

Mal pondered. "Well, I think this Simon sounds exceptional, to take that attitude; I just hope I'd be generous enough to do the same."

"Is that really what you think, Mal?"

"Why?" he countered. "Don't you?"

"I'm not sure . . . I've felt so angry . . . let down resentful, somehow . . . "

"Anyone would, Beatrice! It must have been a terrible shock." Mal was compassionate. "But listen, there's no call to feel bitter — against your mother, or your natural father, or your adopted father. It was just one of those things, at least it worked out okay in the end." She stared at him. He made it sound so simple; was it really as simple as that? "Next thing we need to establish," Mal continued, "is this. Did you really come to Woodstock to locate your father? Are you searching for some roots — is this a major personal quest, or what? If so, why, exactly? What did you have to gain?"

"What did I have to lose?"

Mal smiled slightly, but chose not to reply to this.

She sighed deeply. "You're right, I did come here with the specific intention of finding Jim. I wanted to see him — get to know him — perhaps find out if I had other sisters and brothers . . . "

"Can be dangerous, you know,

stirring up these buried relationships."

"You mean," she said, "I might unearth feelings, or connections, or people, I'd rather not know about?"

"I mean, you have to face all the possibilities. Jim Byrne had that lethal combination, irresistible with irresponsible."

"So this continent might be littered with my half-siblings?"

"Would you mind," Mal wondered, "if it was?"

"Would I have a choice? I don't know what I was hoping! I don't know what I'd feel . . . what I feel . . . " Suddenly, it was all too much for her — the dark secret, the unburdening — and she dissolved into tears.

"Hey, hey, Beatrice! Bear up, keep smiling! Remember what a big girl, a big woman you are? Remember last night? Here, come here, let me hold you, don't weep now, you mustn't weep — here . . . "

Eventually, when he judged her to have recovered, Mal levered her far enough away to search her face. "Got that lot off your chest? Quite a bit of it into *my* chest too, hey?"

"I'm sorry. I feel better now," she gulped. "I needed to tell someone. I'm glad it was you; and I'm still glad it was — like this."

Mal nodded his understanding. Now, climbing out of her own trough with his help, Beatrice noticed that he seemed pale and tense, himself.

"Now," he said, "before we go in and fix us some breakfast — it's my turn for the confessional, yours to make with the sympathetic noises."

"How do you mean?" she sniffed.

"I was trying to tell you this just now, only it didn't quite work out the way I planned. Things aren't that straightforward for me, either; I have something else to confess to *you*."

"More than your suspicion that I was a Byrne all along?"

"To do with that, but more than that."

"Go on, then." She braced herself.

"I told you yesterday about Jim's sister Kerry?"

"The girl you were at school with, who was much younger than him?"

"She looked like him," Mal said, "being his sister. And you look like him, being his daughter. And she and you, both being female . . . "

Light was dawning; a strange cold light. "You mean, I look like her?"

"An uncanny likeness," Mal said. "When I first saw you, sunlit at the door of my workshop, all neat and cool and blonde and lovely, I did a double-take. Reckoned my own dim past had rebounded on me. Reckoned . . . can't say what I reckoned."

"You thought I was Kerry's daughter?"

"Or Kerry herself, come back to haunt me — not that she's dead, as far as I know. No, it was nothing so clear-cut as that; just brought back some, shall we say, highly atmospheric memories . . . "

"You're telling me that you and Kerry — you and my father's sister . . . "

"We had our share, right enough! We got pretty close, as youngsters. We were each other's first, as it happens — both about seventeen — things were kind of free and easy in those days . . . "

He was so complacent! Beatrice was aware of a rising rage; irrational, terrifying, smothering. She couldn't suppress it, and she couldn't control it. She couldn't even, properly, explain it.

"So that's your game! I can see I escaped lightly — I was destined to be just another notch in your cane — carrying on a fine old tradition! Who am I to you, Mal? Who am I really, in all this?"

He frowned. "What are you saying? No need to get so het up!"

"Oh, isn't there? I'm already het up, remember, and this news isn't exactly calculated to make me feel great, is it?" But she didn't feel hot; she felt horribly cold: steel and ice. And the more Mal came over perplexed, the more she hated him.

"Beatrice, I fail to understand why you're taking this line. It was nothing; a youthful affair, over and done by the time we were twenty.

"It went on as long as that? Three years?"

"Two, three . . . I don't know . . . we weren't counting."

"Then she took off and left, married someone else?"

"As a matter of fact, yes."

"And you're trying to pretend you haven't pined for her, ever since?"

"It wasn't that way at all! I've told you about Renata. Renata wiped all that away. Renata was the reality, Kerry was just a . . . "

"Recapturing your lost youth, is that what I'm all about? I knew there must be some reason, some connection that had nothing to do with me! I'll bet you didn't just sleep with Kerry — I'll bet you slept out with her, too, didn't you?"

"Once or twice, maybe — but we all did that, all the time. That has nothing to do with you and me, Beatrice . . . "

But Beatrice wasn't listening to him. She was beside herself. "I'm not me, not actually Beatrice to you at all, am I, Mal? I'm nothing, an empty shell, a hologram — or rather I'm real, but I'm another person, Kerry Byrne, a girl you used to know and love and have fun with? My own father's sister! You saw me coming, decided to use me, for — for — I don't know, some sick attempt to recall the days when you were carefree, before you met Renata, and lost Renata? To — to wipe the slate clean and start all over again? How dare you! How dare you use me that way, Mal? You must have guessed I . . . you knew what it meant to me . . . "

She was sobbing again, flailing out as he tried to grab her — struggling free of his clutches, free of his warm hard body, and his macho cosy sleeping bag, and all it entailed.

"Beatrice! Don't be such a fool! Come back here! Beatrice!"

But she was digging for the rest of her clothes, frantically climbing into them, breathless, deafened, blinded by tears. All at once it was too much, and she was toppled, pushed over the edge . . . conscious only of this obliterating fury, this stabbing blade of betrayal.

Mal recognised someone who was beyond communication. He released her, stood up, quietly got dressed, rolled up the sleeping bags, and waited for her outburst to spend itself, as he was sure it would.

It did, in a way. Five minutes later, she was confronting him at the back door of his house, tear-stained, shaking, exhausted.

"Drive me back to the motel, please, Mal?"

"Sure," he said, "if that's what you want."

"I need . . . it is what I want."

"Okay." He reached in his pocket, took out his wallet and keys. "No breakfast first? Not even coffee?"

"I couldn't. I just need to get — to

be alone. I need to think."

Without a word, he unlocked both doors of his car, got in, and waited for her to join him. During the short drive, neither of them said a word. Beatrice was gradually regaining her equilibrium, but now she just felt stunned — suspended. Outside the motel, she immediately opened her door, grabbed her things, got out and marched off.

"Beatrice!" The summons was sharp, so she turned, despite herself.

He was opening his wallet; through the car window, he was handing her something. "Better not go without what you really came for," he said.

"What?"

"Your father's address."

"My . . . oh, you mean Jim Byrne!"

"I found I still had one for him, in Brooklyn. Must date back a good few years now, though. Can't say whether he'd be still there or not."

"Thanks, I . . . " her voice was hoarse, and she couldn't meet his eye.

But she reached out and took the proffered scrap of paper.

"You could find out the phone number, from Directory," Mal advised.

She nodded, then turned and stumbled away, clutching the paper.

"Beatrice!" She heard him over the purr of the engine. "Don't do anything crazy, will you? You're entitled to be mad at me, for whatever reason you like — whatever peg you want to hang your anger on . . . but don't go over the top, hey?"

Over the top? Clear-headed Beatrice Cole, go over the top?

She swung round to glare at Mal from the steps, but he was already reversing his waggon, then heading away on a squeal of hefty tyres and a cloud of dust.

8

BEATRICE found the house without any trouble at all.

She felt oddly at home in Brooklyn, never having set foot there in her life. Park Slope reminded her of parts of London — or of any British town with a Victorian heritage. Grand terraces, four or five storeys, in mellow grey stone or red brick, with elegant bays, arched windows, carved cornices, balconies. Tree-lined roads; a dappled oasis in the swelter and bustle of New York City.

She found the house, then stood on the pavement for ten minutes, staring up at it. Not quite as smart as some of its neighbours: a bit on the seedy side, in fact, its facade crumbling here, a cracked window there, its stonework in need of attention. But the front door was a defiant red; there were cheerful clean curtains at the windows, and glimpses of a jungle of indoor plants. Encouraged, Beatrice took a deep breath, and one pace towards the front steps.

Then she lost her nerve all over again, turned and fled up the hill. For the next half hour she wandered — along President Street, to Grand Army Plaza with its great gothic arch; back into Prospect Park West, where towering modern blocks nudged and overshadowed quaint period dwellings. Into the Park itself, another green island, soothingly landscaped, haven for strollers, joggers, small children picnicking with their mothers — or their nannies? — like any urban park in any country.

She watched them for a while; then shook herself, sucked in another lungful of fume-laden metropolitan air, and marched herself firmly back to Park Slope.

This time, she neither glanced up at the house, nor hesitated outside, but walked straight up the front steps. There was just one bell, original and imposing, on a pillar to the right of the porch; she rang it.

At first, she thought no one was going to come. The longer she waited, the louder the silence swelled, the more she doubted whether she should be there at all. This was going to be one almighty anticlimax. She prickled and sweated in the midday heat, and was on the someone crossing the hall, fumbling with the latch, opening the door, putting it on the chain . . . then peering through the crack, eyes shaded against the sun — and finally focusing on Beatrice.

"Yes?" The person was tall; the voice was low, but female. Its owner was apparently half-asleep, pushing a mass of brown hair off her pale face, tying the belt of an Oriental silk wrap around her waist.

"I'm sorry, I . . . " Whatever Beatrice had expected, it wasn't this.

"Can I help you?" The young woman

might have been five, six years older than Beatrice; certainly not over thirty. She smiled, took the door off the chain and opened it further. The smile was kind enough, cautiously welcoming even, and laced with a strong hint of curiosity.

"I'm not sure. I . . . I was looking for someone."

"Someone in particular, or would anyone do?"

Now Beatrice returned the smile. "Someone in particular."

"Not me, I presume?"

"That depends who you are," Beatrice pointed out.

"Kitty Flynn. I live in the basement. I guess no one else is in."

"Oh." Beatrice hovered between advance and retreat. What if Mal had been right, after all, and this was a dubious quest, fraught with risks? Should she abandon it, before it got out of hand? Then again, had she travelled so far, covered so much ground, only to shy at this final fence?

"I was hoping," she said, "to find a Mr James Byrne."

Kitty's smile faded to a slight frown; her eyes narrowed on Beatrice's face. "Professor Byrne? You mean Jim Byrne?"

"Professor Byrne, that's it."

The title brought Beatrice an irrational thrill of pride. How aloof and grand it sounded! Yet he was her father, that closest of blood-bonds: this unknown man, this interesting, respected man.

"He — he isn't here any more."

"Oh." Suddenly exhausted, Beatrice leaned on the side of the porch and rubbed her eyes. "Can you tell me where he . . . ?"

"Is it really important?" Kitty interrupted, sharply.

Beatrice glanced up. "Yes! That is . . . yes, it's really important."

Kitty surveyed her for a few seconds. "You'd better come in."

Beatrice nodded her thanks, fighting a sense of foreboding. Inside, it was quiet and dim, in bemusing contrast to the dazzle outside. Blinking, she followed Kitty across a wide hallway. Her canvas shoes made no sound, but Kitty's flip-flops flapped on the mosaic floor tiles.

"My apartment's this way." She led Beatrice through a door, down a winding staircase, through another door. The basement flat was open-plan: one huge room with sleeping area, kitchen corner, living space. French windows opened onto a sunny back yard, from which chaotic plant life appeared to be threatening an unscheduled invasion.

"Sit down — if you can find anywhere." Kitty scooped a couple of dozing cats from her rug-bedecked sofa, and waved a hospitable arm.

"Thanks." Immediately the larger cat — solid, glossy, ginger-and-white — jumped up and made himself comfortable on Beatrice's lap.

"Hey, Fidel! Wait till you're invited!" Kitty admonished.

"No, it's fine. I love cats." Beatrice

stroked Fidel's soft fur, and he purred, kneading her cotton dress, making himself a nest before turning round twice and instantly resuming his slumbers.

Kitty watched him fondly. "Funny how some cats will go to anyone, long as they sit still for two minutes. Fidel's always been one of those, since a kitten. Winnie, now — she's his sister, the little calico one that just disappeared into the yard? She's another can of fish altogether: the suspicious type. She won't come near you unless she knows you real well. Yet they were born into the same litter, both lived with me since they were six weeks old. So much for environment versus genetics!"

"Probably Winnie's more cautious because she's female," Beatrice suggested.

"Right! The female of the species has to be smarter than the male!"

"More discriminating, at least." Beatrice returned Kitty's smile, then added: "I'm sorry if I got you out of bed."

"It's okay — time I was up, anyway. I'm a nurse," Kitty explained. "On the late shift. Came home at five-thirty this morning."

"You must be terribly tired! I really am so sorry I disturbed you!"

"No, it's perfectly fine. I have some studying to do. If I sleep all day, I just feel deadly. Much better to get up now, maybe have a rest later before I go back to work. Coffee — or something cold?"

"Something cold, please."

"Yeah, it's hot, isn't it? One day I'll be able to afford air-conditioning." Kitty moved over to her kitchen area and rummaged in her refrigerator, filled her electric jug, clinked ice in a glass. "Crazy, I know, but I can't start my day without caffeine."

Beatrice was absorbing her surroundings — not least the queen-size double bed. "You live here alone?"

"At the moment. I did have a — partner, for a while, but he left. It didn't work out. We needed our own space, but I still see him."

"I'm sorry, I shouldn't be so nosy."

"I don't mind. It was probably all for the best." Kitty shrugged. "I have fine neighbours upstairs; there's usually someone around if I need moral support . . . it's the immoral sort I'm kind of short on, just now." She chortled.

"But they're all out today, you said?" Beatrice's nerves had been lulled by Kitty's easy warmth, but now they jangled into knots again.

"All out at their day jobs. I'm the only night bird, and that's not all the time. Two weeks on, four off, that's the way we work it."

Kitty crossed the room and handed Beatrice her drink. It was fresh orange juice with soda, long, iced and quenching. Then she went back to the kitchen, poured herself some coffee, and carried it over to a chair, where she sat, sipping thoughtfully. "So — you're British, right?"

"Right." Beatrice was resigned to such instant recognition by now.

"Visiting New York, or working here, or what?"

"Both, in a way. I'll be starting a postgraduate course here soon."

"That's great! And what do I call you?"

"I'm sorry, how rude of me, didn't I say? Beatrice Cole."

"Hi, Beatrice!"

"Hi, Kitty!" Beatrice was amazed at her own lack of inhibition. She might sound unmistakably English, but her native reserve was slipping, here in this informal country, the Land of the Free-and-easy.

"And you came to Park slope hoping to locate Jim Bryne?"

"That's right," Beatrice confirmed, almost reluctantly.

"You have this address for him?"

"Yes, an old friend gave it to me — that is, a new contact of mine . . . an old friend of Jim's."

"Uhuh. Where does this old friend live?"

"Upstate, where Jim came from,"

Beatrice said. "Woodstock, actually. I've just arrived from there."

"You just drove here from *Woodstock*?"

"That's right, I've been there a few days, and . . ."

"This morning? Man, you must be bushed!"

"I'm tired," Beatrice admitted, "but I wanted to make an early start."

"I should say you did! What is it from there — two-and-a-half, three hours? So where are you parked? Outside here?"

"No, I haven't got the car any more. It was hired, and I returned it this morning. I decided it would be more of a nuisance in the city."

"And you could save a heap of money, right?" Beatrice nodded. "But where did you leave all your stuff?" Kitty persisted. "You surely can't be travelling this light from England, via Woodstock?"

"Oh no. I left two bags in a locker at Grand Central Station, till I find somewhere to stay."

"You're here with nowhere to stay?

On your own?" Kitty whistled. "I have to tell you, Beatrice, you're cool."

"I wish I was!" She finished her drink. "But this is helping!"

"You must want to track down Prof. Byrne very much, to make such a trip specially. Couldn't you have tried telephoning first?"

"I did. Directory Enquiries had no record of the name at this address, and there were so many other J. Byrnes listed in New York, I decided to come and see for myself. Anyway," Beatrice lifted her head to meet Kitty's gaze, "I'd finished my business in Woodstock. There didn't seem much point in staying on there any longer."

"They wouldn't have him listed at this address," Kitty said. "Not now."

Beatrice had this feeling she and Kitty were skirting round each other — fending off a challenge. But why should it be a challenge to Kitty? Either she knew Jim's whereabouts, or she didn't. Suddenly, the game had gone on long enough. "*Does* he live here, Kitty?" she demanded.

"He did."

"Did? He moved, then?"

"In away, yes."

"What do you mean, in a way? Didn't he leave a forwarding address?"

"No."

"Oh." Beatrice hesitated, then tried again. "Did you know him?"

"Sure I did! He lived in the top floor apartment. Used to drop in for a drink and a chat — great guy, gregarious, always ready with a laugh . . . we got on real well. He was of Irish extraction, a few generations back, and so am I. 'Couple of crazy Connemara Celts, that's us,' he used to say."

Beatrice smiled. That was Jim; that was how she liked to imagine her father. Popular, full of charm. "Did he live here alone?"

"Most of the time. He had — you know — lady friends, now and then."

"No one permanent? I mean, he must be, well, middle-aged . . . "

"Middle-aged?" Kitty laughed. "He

never acted like a professor, and he never acted his age. He was still lively, good-looking . . . I guess he might have been at least forty, when he . . . forty, going on twenty-one, that was how I thought of him!"

Beatrice was riveted — but they were taking far too long to reach the facts. "When did you last see him?"

Kitty worked it out. "About a year ago."

"And you really don't know where he went, or why?"

"I don't know why. In a way, I do know where." Kitty, normally so animated, had gone very still, stiff; hands tight around her coffee cup.

Beatrice jerked upright, causing Fidel to wake and dig his claws into her knees. "Tell me, then! Kitty, why won't you tell me?"

"I'm trying to, but it's not easy. Whatever you had — have to do with Jim, I have this hunch it's quite a close connection, and . . . "

"And what?"

"And it's a responsibility for me, telling you this."

"Tell me anyway. Please?" Beatrice felt giddy; clammy-cold, then clammy-hot. She lifted the heavy cat from her lap and dumped him unceremoniously on the floor. Unruffled, he padded over to Kitty.

"When he . . . I mean, Jim didn't just leave, Beatrice. What I'm trying to say is, he — he died. I'm sorry! I'm sorry! I knew, I just *knew* it was going to hurt you!" Kitty leaped from her chair and ran to kneel beside Beatrice, one hand on the younger woman s arm.

"He's dead?"

Kitty nodded.

Beatrice registered the words, but their meaning only filtered gradually to her brain, like spring water through thick mud.

She had searched, she had found, and she had lost — all in the same mad moment. She had built up this vivid image of the boy and the man who had been her flesh-and-blood father; now she would never get to see him, in the flesh — hear him, touch him, know him. She could only know what they told her about him, these extraneous individuals who had met him, when she, his daughter, never had — and now never could.

Sharpening the painful irony, her mind produced an echo of Mal's deep voice — so close, so recently, or was it another lifetime? *He may not be your father, strictly speaking, Beatrice — but surely the man who raises you, takes care of you . . . loves you . . . calls himself Dad . . . surely he still has the right to be your father?*

At the time, she had been furious; but from this distance, those words seemed unbearably wise. Mal was right: Jim had never been her flesh-and-blood father, any more than he was today. Jim was dead. Simon existed for her, a three-dimensional reality: the man who called himself Dad. The man she had called Dad, for twenty-one years.

Perhaps she was escaping lightly, after all? Finding the real Jim Byrne would have complicated not only her own life, but also the lives of two people for whom she cared a great deal: Judith and Simon. They had both expressed profound anxiety at the idea, but Beatrice had brushed their apprehensions aside. Now, she understood. To Judith, Jim belonged in a foolish past, no more than a romantic wraith. To Simon, who had never set eyes on him, he was a rival, a threat: his wife's early lover, and now potential usurper of his beloved oldest child's affections. Because Beatrice was his oldest child, she acknowledged that now, even if he had always found it a fraction more difficult to let her know how much he loved her than he had with the other three . . .

Kitty was watching her intently. "Are you all right, Beatrice? I'm real sorry you had to find out this way. Whoever he was . . . "

"He was my father. And don't be

sorry, Kitty — it's not your fault. You did the right thing, telling me, and you did it so kindly . . . "

"He was your *father*?"

"Well, sort of. He was, but he wasn't. I never knew him, but . . . "

"But your mother sure did?"

"So it would seem," Beatrice agreed, with a wry smile.

"And you came to Brooklyn on a private pilgrimage, expecting to dig out some flourishing roots, maybe the odd branch, and all you get is this withered stem?"

"Poetic justice!" Even as she smiled, Beatrice could feel the tears, in her heart, her throat, pricking the back of her eyes. Yes, there had been a loss, and now there would be an emotional effect, instinctive grief, whether she reasoned it away or not. She turned to Kitty. "Can you tell me how it happened? I mean, was he ill, or what?"

"No, he wasn't ill, not so that you'd notice. It was an accident — or so they decided at the inquest."

"There was an inquest? What sort of accident? Car smash?"

"Nothing like that. He-he . . . "

"What, Kitty?"

"You know I told you he lived at the top of this house?" Beatrice nodded. "Well, he took a fall. From the roof."

"He fell off the roof of this house?"

"Died instantly, probably before he hit the ground. They thought he might have just been standing too near the edge, had a dizzy turn, maybe even a mild heart attack, lost his balance, toppled over, rather than . . . "

"Rather than jumping, you mean?"

"I'm sure there was no question of that, Beatrice. Nor of his being pushed. He was alone up there, some eye witnesses saw the whole thing . . . and I told you, he was a cheerful guy, with a rewarding job, a good life, always happy and friendly . . . "

But Beatrice was agitated. "How could anyone be sure he was happy? He might have been lonely, if he could never form lasting relationships . . . if he was still playing the field at forty? Sometimes the most depressed people are the ones who seem the most cheerful."

"I realise that, Beatrice, but I do think it was an accident. I knew him," Kitty reminded her, "and I do. But," she added, gently, "I realise you can never know for sure."

They sat in silence; then, abruptly, Beatrice said: "Is it easy to get out on the roof?"

"Sure. There's a door, just near the door of his — that is, what used to be his apartment. It's not locked. I like to sit out there and sunbathe. The view's something else! You can see the whole city, Manhattan, and beyond. Mind you, after the accident, none of us went out there for a while, but life has to go on . . . "

"Lightning doesn't strike twice in the same place?"

"We keep well away from the edge, let me tell you. And the owners of the house put a kind of low fence up, all the way round. Not that we'd need reminding." Assured that Beatrice was coping with the trauma, Kitty allowed herself a brief recalling shudder.

"Were you there when . . . I mean, did you see . . . ?"

"Oh, no, I was out at work. By the time I got home, there was nothing to be seen. The couple in the first floor apartment, Ben and Monica, they told me about it in the evening. They were very good, gave me a drink, talked to me . . . we talked half the night, I seem to remember. Death brings folk closer together like nothing else in life."

"So, we could go out there now?" Beatrice pressed

"You want to go out there? You sure?"

"I want to see it — the exact place — please! If you could take me?"

Kitty considered, then stood up and stretched. "Okay, if that's what you want. Just let me get some clothes on and go to the bathroom."

Five minutes later, in shorts and t-shirt, she led Beatrice out of her subterranean den, upstairs to the entrance hall; then more stairs; and more; and more . . . until at last they pushed open a heavy fireproofed door at the very top, and found themselves on the roof.

It shimmered with heat, reflected off the silver insulating material which lined it. It was punctuated with lumps and protrusions: chimneys and cowls, heating and air-conditioning outlets, aerials and ventilation shafts. Beyond, all around, as Kitty had promised, this stupendous urban vista: more rooftops; then out across the great city, grey, with soothing patches of green; jagged and sculptured, teeming with invisible crowds; then on out to the sea . . .

Beatrice stood, transfixed; then she faced Kitty. "Where, exactly?"

From a safe spot at the centre of the roof, Kitty pointed to the front of the house. "Over there. Be careful, Beatrice!"

Beatrice walked steadily to the edge, easily climbed the low barrier, crouched, and peered carefully down. She saw everyday life, not death: peaceful pavements, streets, the leafy tops of trees, miniature cars, occasional foreshortened pedestrians. She saw no ghost, no flashback, no action replay — no sign of the stark fact that her father had lived just there, stood just there, and died just there, twelve months before. She received no mystic message across the ether, no clue as to how it had really happened. She didn't know, and she never would.

She sighed, shut her eyes tight, opened them again — and screwed them up in a frown. It seemed she might be experiencing some kind of flashback after all; the intensity of heat and shock, no doubt. That beefy vehicle — the one which had just pulled up opposite the house — it recalled, with a sick jolt, the Cameronmobile. Of course it couldn't be; simply a trick of light and memory. Now it had disappeared beneath the awning of trees. More than likely, she'd hallucinated it.

She stood up — too quickly. She was short of sleep and sustenance, overwhelmed, overheated. The roof spun, and so did the scene below. She lurched sideways a step, hearing Kitty's voice calling out to her as if through a dense fog . . . then she pulled all her strength together, and lurched a step back . . . and painfully, another . . . until she stumbled against the low fence, tumbled over it, and collapsed in a heap on the scorching roof, trembling, panting, her head still whirling, her stomach churning.

Kitty came dashing over to her. "Beatrice! What happened? Are you okay? I knew this was a terrible idea! Beatrice!"

The world stopped spinning; her insides calmed down. Feebly, she raised her head; then gradually the rest of her. Tottering to her feet, she allowed Kitty to support her, and together they made slow progress, back through the door into the house, and down the endless stairs.

As they approached the entrance hall, it became clear that the peace of the house was being rudely shattered. First a vigorous banging, then a strident peal on the bell, then further resounding thumps.

"What now?" Kitty leaned Beatrice against a wall, then went over to open the front door before it caved in under the onslaught. She put it on the chain, just as she had when Beatrice arrived, and peered round it.

"Hey, man, no need to bust our door down! What can we do for you?"

"I apologise," a male voice rumbled. "I couldn't make myself heard, and it's extremely important. I'm looking for someone, and I have reason to believe they might be . . . "

"Another lost soul, looking for someone!" Kitty called over her shoulder, to Beatrice. "Seems like you're all out, today!"

Beatrice was using her last ounce of energy to heave herself away from this supporting wall, and — and what?

Make a sensible getaway bid? Or rush headlong, headstrong, in the direction of the voice?

It was, of course it was, Mal Cameron. It had been no hallucination, but Mal Cameron's station waggon. Jim Byrne might not obligingly appear to her at the spot where he died; but Mal Cameron was here, large as life and twice as unexpected. How? Why?

"I'm looking for a Miss Cole." He was now regaling Kitty with his most persuasive charm. "I thought she might be here."

"Beatrice Cole?" Kitty scratched her head, then shot an enquiring glance back at Beatrice — who could only shrug and lean on her wall, fighting this impossible conflict, hostility tempered with relief.

"That's the lady. She's been here, then?"

"What if she has? Who wants to see her?"

"The name's Cameron," said Cameron.

Kitty stayed where she was, but declared, in stentorian tones that echoed through the hall and out of the door, "Beatrice! There's this tall good-looking type out here, asking for you. Has a beard, calls himself Cameron. You know him? You want to see him?"

Beatrice managed to convey her confusion by shaking and nodding her head at the same time. Then she opened her mouth, but no sound came out. Then she tried again, and a pathetic squeak did emerge.

"Yes, I know him. You can let him in. I — I'll see him."

Kitty obediently unchained the door, and stood back to allow an unobstructed Cameron entry. He strode in, caught sight of Beatrice, and headed straight for her. Paralysed, she simply waited. As he reached her, his arms came out to her, and she knew that her own were lifting to him, whether her mind gave them permission or not.

"Beatrice! You look awful! What the hell have you been playing at?"

"Thanks a lot . . . I came . . . oh, Mal!" His hands, his voice, his eyes — his whole self expressed such care and concern, that she crumpled. She let go of her protecting wall, and fell forward, against him.

"Idiot woman! I know you're crazy, but when I gave you this address I never thought you'd do anything this far-out! I thought at least you'd phone first, not take right off for New York!"

"I did try, but . . . " But her words were mumbled, lost against him.

"I gave you an hour to cool off," he told her. "Then I went back to the motel. Solly said you'd checked out straight away and left, without breakfast. I know how you were feeling, but I couldn't believe you'd do that, Beatrice, before seeing me . . . "

"Oh, Mal!" She'd been so enraged; so confident she was doing the right thing — the only thing — walking out of his life forever.

Discreetly, Kitty coughed. "I hate to

interfere in such a touching reunion, but would someone care to tell me what's going down?"

Strength was returning to Beatrice, magically seeping in through her pores. She felt restored enough to push Mal away, then smile ruefully at Kitty. "I'm sorry, Kitty. Mal — Malcolm Cameron is a friend of mine, from Woodstock. He guessed where I was going, because he was the one who gave me this address."

"He's the — old contact you mentioned? Jim Byrne's old friend?"

"He's the one. Mal, this is Kitty Flynn, who's been really kind . . . "

"Ms Flynn." Mal detached himself from Beatrice, long enough to shake Kitty's hand. Then he said, "Jim Byrne's still around here, then?"

The two women stared at him, then at each other.

"Let's all go down to my apartment," suggested Kitty. "I could use some breakfast, and I suspect you could too, Beatrice. I'll go out for some bagels, while you tell Mal — whatever you want to tell him. Okay?"

"Thanks, Kitty. That sounds great."

While Kitty ran on ahead, Mal and Beatrice followed at a more sedate pace, his arm firmly about her waist — sharing a silence which bristled with untied ends and unanswered questions.

9

KITTY was right: Beatrice's spirits were much revived by a pile of fragrant blueberry muffins, crisp poppy-seed bagels, and creamy coffee.

"A fine American tradition," Mal commented, through a mouthful. "All our most important meetings take place over brunch."

Kitty's back was turned to them as she organised the coffee-pot. "And is this a most important meeting?" she wondered, innocently.

Mal's eyes were on Beatrice's face, but she kept hers lowered. She felt so bewildered, she couldn't even tell what she did feel. Mal seemed to know her so deeply, so quickly. Finding her fled from Woodstock, he had instantly guessed where and why — and more disconcertingly, he had cared, enough to come hurtling after her. Now he knew the sad outcome of her impetuous trail, because she had filled in the details, as succinctly as she could, while she rested on Kitty's sofa.

What Kitty couldn't be expected to fathom was the precise nature of this dramatic relationship, though Beatrice reckoned she'd be having a good try. Now, as if sensing their brief awkwardness, Kitty continued: "It could be a lucky meeting between *us*, Beatrice."

"How do you mean?"

Kitty came over, brandishing the coffee pot. "Well, *I'm* glad we met, even if you aren't!"

"I'm sorry!" Beatrice flushed. "Of course I'm glad! I just . . . "

"Hey, it's okay, I don't offend that easily! I'm a Brooklyn girl, born and bred, remember? My hide's pretty tough. But I'm not that insensitive, either; I do understand this morning hasn't exactly been an unqualified success, from where you're sitting.

I do realise it's not every day you find and lose a father in the same five minutes."

"I know you do," Beatrice said, "and you've been wonderful. If I hadn't found you here . . ."

"You might have gone away again, and never learned the awful truth."

"Oh, I'd have come back, you can be sure of that! I'd have kept coming back until I did find someone here."

"She would, too," Mal observed.

"Sure she would. So would I, in her place. Another muffin?" Kitty passed the plate. Mal took one, but Beatrice shook her head. "What I was trying to say," Kitty went on, "was that it's good that we met, because at least now you know someone with a pad in New York. When you start college, and you need to look for an apartment, you can always crash here until you find somewhere of your own."

"That's really kind of you!"

On learning the truth about Jim, Beatrice had allowed those few shocked tears to escape. Then, this cold numbness. But now, she felt herself thawing out, under the influence of these two people — of Mal's eyes, constantly on her, and Kitty's spontaneous generosity.

"Offers like that don't grow on trees," Mal said. "Especially Big Apple trees," he added.

"They certainly don't. Thanks, Kitty."

"You're welcome. You'd be welcome, any time. You can see there's not much space, but I'd enjoy the company. So don't forget, Beatrice — right away, today even, if you have nowhere else to go from here . . . "

"I . . . " Beatrice began.

Mal stepped calmly out of his audience role, and took charge. "She won't need to trespass on your hospitality any more today, thanks all the same, Kitty. She has somewhere to stay tonight."

"Oh, I have, have I?" Beatrice rounded on him. She'd been surprisingly pleased to see him here, but Woodstock had served its purpose; she had seen quite enough of the place for the time being.

Mal didn't flinch. "Sure you have — if you'll accept my invitation to spend a couple of days in my apartment."

"Your . . . ?" Beatrice squeaked.

"You have a place in Brooklyn?" Kitty regarded Mal in a new light.

"Not Brooklyn. Greenwich Village."

"As well as this . . . upstate estate I've been hearing about?"

"It's only a small penthouse," said Mal, modestly.

"A penthouse! Wow!" Kitty was impressed.

"I have to see people in the city all the time, in connection with my work," Mal explained. "When I come up, I need a place to drop anchor."

"That figures. But a penthouse!"

"I haven't been there in quite a while, as it happens." Mal's expression hardened; he stared away, out of the window. "As a matter of fact, this is my first visit to the city in — in a few months."

He bent to salute Winnie, who had padded in from the yard, headed straight for Mal, and wound her sinewy tortoiseshell form round his legs.

"Would you look at that, Beatrice!" Kitt crowed. "Didn't I tell you this cat's finicky about who she goes to? So what does this guy have, that none of my other visitors have?"

Beatrice watched Mal's broad hand, those long tactile fingers, stroking the sleek fur — under the chin, behind the ears, down the ridged back. When she spoke, her voice came out husky. "Butter on his fingers?" she suggested.

Kitty laughed. "There has to be more to it than that."

"Cats have a way of knowing when you need *them*," Mal contributed. "They don't care to show how much they need *you*, but if they feel someone has a vulnerability, that's different."

Kitty was intrigued, but it was hardly her place to probe. She didn't know either of these fascinating folk well enough yet, nor understand what tensions shifted between them, or why. Or quite what they had to do with Beatrice's father, poor Jim Byrne. But she liked both of them, and, avid student of human nature as she was, she resolved to work on it.

She started bustling, carrying cups and plates over to the kitchen area. "It's always good to meet another cat freak," was all she said.

Beatrice was glad to help her. "Where's Fidel?"

"He went out on the town. He'll be back for his scraps, soon as he's near enough to smell bagels. He just loves buttered rolls."

Mal had wandered over to the French doors. Now he stood, hands in the pockets of his jeans, gazing out. Because his back was turned, his voice came as an invisible summons, hitting the far corner of the room, ricocheting off the walls, back to where the women stood near the sink.

"Beatrice?"

"What?" She paused, in the act of drying a knife.

He wheeled round. "You haven't given me an answer.

"What was the question?" she hedged.

"How about spending a couple of days at my place in Greenwich?"

Beatrice put down the knife and the cloth, and walked slowly towards him. A few feet away, she stopped. "I'm just not sure, Ma . . . "

"First, you need to rest up," he said. "Then I thought we might hit the town — the full tourist bit. The Trade Center . . . Chinatown . . . Central Park . . . Broadway good old Liberty . . . how about it?" As he spoke, his voice softened, from challenge to introspection. "I can't remember how long it is since I really saw any of those places." His gaze was straying from Beatrice, to some space within himself. "Saw them properly, I mean, not just in the background. And I could show you some of the big art galleries, and the smaller ones where I . . . "

"Sounds good to us, hey Winnie?" Kitty was addressing the cat, of course, but her comment wafted over to them.

Beatrice was frowning, and so was Mal. Then, all at once, she was smiling — and so was Mal.

"It does sound good. It sounds like a fine idea. Thanks, Mal," she said, "I'd like that very much."

His message reached her, plain enough, and fair enough. He'd materialised, the White Knight, a mercy dash of over a hundred miles to help her out of this self-imposed jam. But he had his own needs, too. Tentatively, he was asking for her help in his own process of rehabilitation. And suddenly, it seemed the least she could do.

"That's great! I'm sure you won't regret it," he said.

"I'm sure you won't," came the Greek chorus from the kitchen regions.

"Maybe you'll join us for a meal, Kitty? I know this great place in Little Italy. The owner's a friend of mine."

"Pasta is absolutely my favourite!"

Kitty grinned across at him. "Only thing is, I'm on nights," she added regretfully.

"So we'll have lunch! What do you think Beatrice? Tomorrow?"

"Tomorrow sounds good." Beatrice sat down, rather abruptly, on the nearest chair. "But before I do anything else, I'll have to catch up on some sleep. I'm sorry, I seem . . . " she yawned.

Kitty came over to her. "You've had a real tough morning: you must be wiped out. Want to use my bed for a while?"

Before Beatrice could reply, Mal was in charge again. "Thanks, Kitty, but I think it might be best if we pick up her stuff from Grand Central right away, then head to my place. She'd be in your way here. I can tuck her up in a quiet corner, where she can stay spark out for as long as she wants. How does that grab you, Beatrice? All right?"

"Yes. Please." She could only mutter, and nod, and yawn again. "I'm sorry, I can't understand why I'm so . . . I'm not usually . . . "

"Nervous exhaustion," said Kitty and Mal, in unison. All three of them smiled at one another; then Mal helped Beatrice to her feet.

Kitty scribbled her telephone number on an old envelope and handed it to Beatrice, who shoved it into her purse. The two women exchanged a hug; then, without further words, Beatrice plodded off on the trek upstairs, without waiting for Mal, without even glancing back for him.

Through the cool hall, out into the garish afternoon sunshine; down the steps, into the quiet hot street, where she could see the Cameron mobile, waiting under an umbrella of trees. As she went, she pondered. In a short, fairly conventional lifetime, she had made comparatively few close friends. Not (she now understood) *really* close. Such was her natural reserve, even after years of knowing a person, she rarely let them right into her affections, trusted them. Yet today, in this bizarre situation, after a few brief hours, she had — she sensed it — acquired a friend who truly was a friend. Another woman whom she could relax with, confide in, turn to.

Just as yesterday, even more extraordinarily, she had acquired . . . her mind blanked off from the word, but she forced herself to face it. She had acquired a lover — because Mal was surely that, whether things ever progressed any further or not. She sighed. He might hope to be, or become, her lover; but was he also her friend? That might be more crucial, in the end — and it remained to be seen. The attraction was there, sure enough, powerful, mutual; but was it personal, aimed at the real Beatrice, or symbolic? He had been Kerry Byrne's lover, too, all those years ago, and surely her friend as well. Was Beatrice no more than a reincarnation of that youthful affair? Looking so like Kerry, as she apparently did? Could she ever know?

Anyway, why did it matter?

It did matter: that was why she had run away! But she was too tired now to work out how much it mattered, or what she should do about it. As she crossed the street, Mal caught up with her and took her arm. He said nothing as he ushered her into his car, then got in and started the engine. His attention was fixed on the road; his profile set, not harsh, but masked. She guessed he was no less preoccupied, abstracted, than she was.

Gratefully, she leaned back on the seat and closed her eyes.

* * *

It was an elderly apartment block, eight storeys, quite low by modern standards. Nothing too pretentious, but with its own courtyard out the back, its own janitor, even its private parking lot: a rare privilege at the heart of any metropolis.

They took the vintage elevator up to the top floor. Although she knew it was irrational, Beatrice was nervous in lifts; but this was the least alarming kind, with folding doors which let you see where you were going. And it helped that Mal was there, unperturbed as he operated it, then leaned back in a corner, whistling softly under his breath.

Beatrice told herself that was even more irrational. Being stuck in a lift with Mal might prove more fraught than being stuck in one alone.

His penthouse was no larger than Kitty's basement, and almost as open-plan. After that, resemblances were few and far between. It was fully, blessedly air-conditioned, for a start. And so bright; such a sense of space, the outside flooding in through wide picture windows! Unlike Kitty's, it was impeccably tidy. Tastefully furnished, enhanced with contemporary works of art, certainly impressive and doubtless worth a fortune — but not exactly lived-in. A showpiece, rather than a home.

Mal stood in the middle of his living-room, assessing her reactions.

"They come in and clean twice a week, keep an eye on things. It's a waste, really; I haven't used this place in months. Even when Renata was alive, we only came when we had to. Since she died, I haven't . . . " He turned away, biting his lip, before concluding, "I have no incentive, no reason to be here. Who do I need to see? I might as well lock myself up in Woodstock and work on my project, till it's finished."

"Anyone would understand that, Mal." Beatrice had wandered over to the window, drawn like a moth to the light — mesmerised, even in her drained state, by this prospect of Village and Park, again the study in grey and green. "But it's wonderful here! You're very lucky."

"I know that, Beatrice."

"And kind," she heard herself saying,

"to share it with me. And — and to come rushing after me, all this way, when you discovered I'd disappeared." She went on contemplating the view, and she had to clear an obstruction from her throat, but she persevered. "I want to thank you for that, Mal, and say I'm sorry I left without telling you, and I — I do appreciate this, whatever . . . "

As she spoke, he had silently crossed the room behind her. She jumped as he loomed beside her, also gazing out. "Whatever my evil ulterior motives?"

"Whatever I might have accused you of, when I left you this morning."

"You still regret what's already happened between us, Beatrice?"

"I didn't say that. I just said . . . "

"Then you don't regret it?"

"I didn't say that, either!" Her brain wasn't at its quickest.

"I hope you don't regret it," he said, gently. "Because I don't, and believe me, it's no more significant for you than it is for me."

"If you say so." He kept his distance, but she felt his eyes on her.

"You're still paranoid about its true significance for me, aren't you, Beatrice?"

"Can you blame me?" she snapped.

"It was all fine, until I let slip how much you remind me of Kerry, wasn't it? Then you decided, because you resemble my first girlfriend — which is hardly surprising, since she happened to be your aunt — that I'm not really interested in you at all — that this has to be some pathetic attempt to dig up ancient juvenile passions. Now listen, Beatrice, I know how traumatised you are by what you've just learned; but before we go any further, I have to say this: you can't be thinking straight, if you can really think that!"

A note of controlled anger had invaded his voice. Beatrice responded with an irritation of her own; then — unexpectedly — it ebbed clean away.

She had misjudged him, of course.

Through her exhaustion, she perceived the truth with an odd clarity. And the truth was, she was no more Mal's victim than he was hers.

Learning of her resemblance to Kerry had come at a critical moment. Beatrice had been only too ready to fix on a scapegoat for her own understandable tension. The night had been magic; nothing to lead to shame, or regrets, perhaps — but dawn had brought the inevitable doubt, the acute sense of exposure. Then Mal had presented her with this untoward twist, and she had seized on it, twisted her fears tightly into it.

While she sifted through this painful realisation, then her responses to it, Mal was speaking again, his tone softer this time. "I'm not saying you didn't give me plenty to think about. While I drove here, I was working it out all the way; searching my soul, my conscience, to see if you were even a bit right. About Kerry, I mean. I have to admit, Beatrice, I can't rule it out completely.

I mean, how can a person ever be sure, when it comes to the whys and wherefores of wanting another person? Do you understand every particle of why you chose *me*?"

"Mal, I do know what you mean . . . "

But he was into his stride. "I was as tough with myself as I could be; put myself in your place, worked it through, and I can only tell you this: yesterday, last night, I was aware of nothing but you, the way you were . . . the way you are. I never thought of you as anyone but Beatrice, I never wanted you as anyone but Beatrice. If you can accept that . . . "

"I can. I can accept that," she whispered. "I'm sorry . . . "

"Don't be sorry! You have nothing to apologise for, Beatrice, any more than I do! I take full responsibility for my actions, as you do for yours — and all the murky motivations behind them. I thought we should clear that out of the way; clear the air before we continue this — this relationship, friendship, whatever the hell it is. Okay?"

She nodded. And at last, she tore her eyes from the view, and faced up to Mal; his challenge, his reality, her feelings about that reality.

"Okay. I admit — this morning I was suddenly afraid. I suddenly realised what I'd — what we'd done, or nearly done — so when you gave me the idea about Kerry, I thought I could hang some of my responsibility on that. Push it over onto you, so I could safely escape . . . "

"Which is precisely what you then tried to do," he pointed out.

He was taking such care not to touch her. But his smile was heart-stopping, a physical heat — so that she stepped back, out of its range of influence. Only of course that influence was elastic, and stretched after her, as it would have continued to do if she had retreated to the opposite end of the apartment. "Without much success," she said.

"You made your point. You brought

this problem out in the open. I respect you for that." He was moving closer. She did not back off, but tiredness had mysteriously evaporated — or transformed itself into another, very different, even more urgent craving. Her uncertainty had evaporated along with it, and all she wanted was to be in his arms. To lose herself in them, in him, all over again.

It was a new, pure longing, and it swept through her, so that she held her breath and shut her eyes. After a brief, interminable silence, she opened them. He had halted, millimetres and yet miles away.

"Now," he was smiling, "before you collapse in a heap at my feet, did we say something about resting up? I have plans for us this evening. I won't drag you too far, but I thought we might eat Mexican. There's this place not far from here, on Charles Street. That suit you?"

"I — I don't know. I've never tried Mexican."

"Then it's time you did. What's more," Mal said, "it's time I took the plunge — it used to be one of Renata's favourites, so I've been avoiding it, along with so many things we used to do together. Now you're here to do them with me; a gift, instant therapy. Isn't that my real ulterior motive, Beatrice?" he added, softly. "Isn't that what I really need you for? Forget all that garbage about Jim Byrne's sister; that was stale, old, a pickled red herring. Renata was alive and warm; now she isn't — but I am, and you are."

Before Beatrice could field this new line of attack, he had grabbed her hand and pulled her away from the window, across the room, through a curtained arch into the bedroom. There was only the one bedroom, and most of that was filled with the one bed — of true New World proportions, at least seven feet wide, but still only the one of it. Mal dropped her hand, and threw back the brocaded bedspread, richly multicoloured, revealing pristine white sheets.

"I told them to always keep it ready for me, just in case I ever made it back to the city." He returned to the living-room, indicating the ensuite bathroom as he went. "Feel free to take a shower," he called, over his shoulder. "There should be plenty of soap and clean towels in there. Then sleep as long as you like."

"Thanks," she called back. "Where — what will you be doing?"

He reappeared, carrying her bags, which he dumped on the bed. "Me? Oh, I'll probably put my feet up, too. My settee's reasonably comfortable, out there. I often used to lie on it and meditate." He folded his arms and leaned against the wall. "You're not the only one who had a short and broken night, remember?"

"I remember." She bent to unzip one of her cases.

"I do like the way you blush, Beatrice," he said. "It's so British!"

She supposed it was more of a compliment than an insult — just; and suddenly she was tottering; too weary to care. That rekindling of — whatever it was: desire? surely not love? — had waned as fast as it had waxed. Now all she wanted was to get her body horizontal, her mind empty for a few hours. To build up some resources, perhaps defences, against whatever Mal planned to throw at her next.

10

FIVE days later, they were in Mal's car again, heading upstate.

They exchanged few words or glances. Their silence had been peaceful, amicable; now it was filled to bursting with rock music from one of Mal's much-played library of cassettes. This one was intimately familiar to Beatrice, yet for the moment she couldn't pin it down.

"Lost dreams and found dreams in America, in America, in America," the male singer chanted, to an accompaniment of plangent electric guitar. "Lost dreams and found dreams in America, in America, in America . . . "

Beatrice coasted on the flowing current of it, the hypnotic repetition of lyrics and melody. Then, in the ensuing pause, she turned to Mal.

"Who was that?"

"Van Morrison, of course."

"Of course! I should have remembered — he's one of my mother's favourites. She's always playing that album. *Wavelength*, isn't it?"

"That's the one. Nippy music, hey? I'm not surprised: it's around her generation, and that track could be her theme tune."

And mine? Beatrice almost added; but she contented herself with a wry smile, settling back in her seat. She might as well make the most of being a passenger, free to relax and enjoy the passing scenery. She had never intended to return to Woodstock, but Mal urgently wanted her to, for reasons best known to himself. He had built up the pressure, day by day, until last night she had acquiesced. Now, the farther north they got, the more quietly enigmatic Mal grew, the more Beatrice tensed up.

In all, it had been a strange, suspended five days, riddled with contradictions. To be precise, five days and six nights.

The days and evenings had been upbeat; spent, true to Mal's promise, exploring New York City. Under his expert guidance, she felt she knew it — if anyone could expect to know such a complex tangle of styles, atmospheres, races, classes, occupations, after so short a time. They had walked and talked, wined and dined, sampled high culture and low fun, shopping and sightseeing, until her head whirled and her feet ached on the baking pavements. They had been drenched in violent downpours, when the humid heat finally cracked and crashed in electric storms.

Mal had introduced her to a few friends and colleagues, cautiously at first, but with increasing confidence, so that Beatrice glowed with pleasure, aware that she was fulfilling his profound need — enabling his reinstatement in society. On her own account, she was growing increasingly bewildered; but she was glad for his sake.

The first day, as arranged, they had shared pizza and pasta with Kitty, in what turned out to be one of Woody Allen's favourite haunts; another anecdote which Beatrice mentally noted to tell Simon and Judith, who were avid Woody fans, and had seen each of his films at least twice. Kitty had repeated her invitation to Beatrice to stay with her any time, and they had parted on terms of easy affection.

After that, she and Mal had eaten every species of exotic fare, from Chinese *dim sum* to Spanish *paella*. Fortunately it was too hot to manage much at a time, or Beatrice was sure her stomach would be complaining, not to mention expanding. They had never run dry of lively conversation, though they kept it carefully general, by mutual consent. There was plenty of laughter, but occasionally Beatrice became conscious of a sadness, deep within herself. A sudden inner lurch, a clench of unresolved bitterness about the secret past of a mother she'd thought she knew so well; a father she'd belatedly discovered, only to find his image fading before it could be made flesh.

As for Mal, he had gone the other way: relaxed, unwound, before her very eyes. Transformed himself into this perfect companion, keeping it up through every day and evening — witty, light-hearted, yet serious and considerate when necessary.

And the nights? They were a very different story. The nights hadn't been a problem, exactly; they had been — how could she put it? An anticlimax? A non-event? A puzzle? A disappointment? A relief?

The honest fact was, they had been a perplexing blend of all these ingredients. That first night, for example, after her afternoon rest and a convivial evening, Beatrice hadn't felt particularly tired; she'd felt hyped up, ready for further shared expressions and discoveries.

But when it came to bedtime, Mal had simply undressed, climbed into the other side of the vast bed, leaned across to smile and plant a chaste kiss on her forehead, rolled over to his patch at the far edge — about a mile away — curled up, and within three minutes, fallen fast asleep.

This pattern had been repeated on subsequent nights, until it had become so predictable, Beatrice neither expected nor hoped for anything else. Or if she did, she had too much self-respect, and too little experience, to risk such an admission to herself, still less to Mal.

It was logical enough, after all. She should be pleased: wasn't he merely proving they could be friends, not just lovers? There was only the one bed, and it was such a generous one. Plenty of room for two tired people after an exhausting but rewarding day, however platonic their status. So why should either of them be banished to the sofa? No, if this was how he wanted it — and presumably, he must assume she wanted it — it made excellent sense. Each night, lying beside him, yet so far from him, Beatrice counselled herself that she ought to be grateful. She normally liked things to make excellent sense.

Once every twenty-four hours, without fail, Mal asked her if she'd had enough of the fast lane and the bright lights for a while. "I wouldn't want you to stay on here just for my sake," he said, the third evening.

"I'm having a fantastic time, Mal. Why — aren't you?"

"You know it's doing me an amazing amount of good, Beatrice," he said.

"Is it your work? You feel you should get back to your — project?"

"Nothing like that," he insisted. "I just thought you might feel like coming back to Woodstock for a while, before your semester starts."

"Why should I?" she parried. "There's nothing for me there — not now I've learned about Jim. That was all I went there for."

"It may be all you went for, but it

wasn't all you found," had pointed out. "Are you sure you're not just scared of what else you might find — or feel — if you went back? Don't you still have some unfinished business there?"

"I can't think what you're getting at!" she had retorted.

"Listen, Beatrice," he said, "we had us one magical day and night there together, you and I. But how about our private, personal ghosts — yours and mine? Don't they deserve the chance to get laid?"

She ignored his cryptic pun. "But I'm really enjoying being here, Mal; I don't feel like going back to Woodstock."

He shrugged. "If being here makes you feel safer," he said.

But the next evening, he tried again. And the next, with similar results. The more he pushed, the harder Beatrice dug in, though she scarcely knew why herself. It became a battle between them, but with no winner or loser, no violence or bloodshed, not so much as a raised voice. Every evening, he brought the topic up, and she turned his suggestion down flat; every night, he climbed into bed the far side, bestowed on her a sweet smile, a sweeter kiss on the cheek — and immediately fell asleep.

But on the sixth evening, his mood was different; brittle.

"Tomorrow, I really do have to go back," he declared.

"Your work?"

"No, not my work. Not the way you mean," he said.

"Why, then?"

"I can't tell you, but I assure you it's vital. Please, Beatrice?"

"But why is it so vital that I should come with you, Mal? I could stay on up here with Kitty. You know she said I could, any time, and I ought to be thinking about looking for somewhere to live when . . ."

"Time enough for all that. I've told you, we both have unfinished business to see to first, together, and it has to be in Woodstock."

"And it has to be tomorrow?"

"Absolutely. Sorry. No other day will do."

Suddenly, her curiosity won over her obstinacy, and she found herself nodding, conceding — probably surprising herself even more than him.

So Mal was having his way; and here they were, next morning, on the road north. Beatrice wondered what tricks he had up his sleeve. Whatever came of this budding relationship, she had certainly never known — never imagined — one like it. It seemed so endlessly varied, so tautly strung between tension and serenity.

They arrived at Mal's house in time for lunch. Then they headed straight for Wilson State Park, and spent a carefree afternoon splashing in the lake and basking on the grass. They rubbed suntan oil into each other's backs; apart from that, they kept a safe distance. If either of them felt stirring echoes of that other watery explosion, up at North Lake, they showed nothing. At least, Beatrice showed nothing; and these days, what Mal was actually feeling was anyone's guess.

Later, Mal cooked them steaks for supper in his own kitchen, with evident pleasure at being home again. As the hours drew into evening, he became more and more distracted. Beatrice watched him, wondering what was passing through his mind; also wondering where she was expected to sleep, now they were sharing a house with at least three bedrooms.

At about six, Mal disappeared for five minutes and reappeared with a bundle of — among other items — bedding. She eyed it suspiciously.

"That," she said, "looks like those old sleeping bags."

"Thought you'd recognise your pals," he said.

"And is there some good reason for their return to the scene?"

"An excellent reason," he assured her. "We might need them."

"Tonight?"

"This evening, at any rate," he said.

"Why?" Her heart quickened, despite herself. "You're not plotting another *al fresco* night in your field?"

"Not there, no."

"Then where are we going?"

"You'll know — when we get there." He put the bundle down, and came up to her. His voice dropped, to a tone she hadn't heard since they were last here together. "If we get there. This is not a kidnap, Beatrice. I'm not hijacking you; I'm humbly asking you to come."

"But how can I answer, if you won't tell me where?"

"You'll have to trust me, won't you?"

He reached out to trail one fingertip down her cheek, coming to rest lightly on her mouth. It was his first such gesture in so long, she gasped at the sheer impact of it. Why fool herself? This had simmered, deep inside both of them — a submerged turbulence, through these limbo days. She had the fancy that Mal was offering her a flame for a dormant fuse on a powder-keg; he held out the match, but she must agree to strike it, on equal terms with him.

"Will we be staying out all night?"

"Not necessarily. It depends. Just an hour or two, maybe."

She stared at him. He was solemn, tender, supremely calm. For once she obeyed her instincts, rather than her reason. "Okay, Mal," she whispered. "I'll come, wherever it is."

"That's my girl! Let's be off, then, or it'll be too late. Wrap up well — you'll need your sweater, that's right. Here, take these." He was thrusting part of the bundle into her arms, grabbing the rest, striding on ahead, out to the drive.

"Too late for what?" She ran to catch up with him but he was well ahead of her, already loading the equipment into his car.

This time, as he drove, their silence was packed with messages — strident, yet incoherent — punctuated with question marks and exclamation marks.

Not far out of Woodstock, he turned off onto a smaller road. Then they were climbing, and Beatrice's agitation rose with the altitude. The hill steepened — up through trees, a few at first, thickening to woods, then out the other side, to a plateau near the top of a swooping summit. She could just make it out in the half-light, looming above them, sloping away to a spreading vista of shape and shadow.

Trees, houses; land, water, mapped out below them. All in the negative, emptied of colour in the descending dusk.

Abruptly, Mal swung the car off the road, onto a patch of rough ground, sheltered behind thick bushes, and switched off the engine.

"Don't you know where this is?"

"No?" Her own voice startled her — husky, uncertain.

"Overlook."

"Overlook Mountain?"

"Right. You've seen it from below, haven't you?"

"I did locate it, my first evening — I wanted to see where . . . "

"Where it all happened, between Jim and Judith?" Mal said. "Where you were conceived? Yes, I know, Beatrice."

"It's — er, high, isn't it?" she squeaked, feeling foolish.

"High enough. We always used to say, there she was, good old Overlook, keeping watch, checking up on us . . . but if we climbed up here, near the top — well, then we were right under her nose; too close for her to see what we did."

"We?"

"All of us kids."

"You and Kerry?"

"I might have brought Kerry up here, once or twice, sure. After I was old enough to drive, and if I could borrow a car."

Beatrice considered this barb, and found she could accept it without so much as a pang. So, here was one ghost that had already been successfully laid.

But Mal was right: there were others, more subtle, more threatening, which she had been keeping firmly at bay, and which did need exorcising, before she could go forward in any direction.

She drew a deep breath. "You think Jim thought that, too? About escaping from Overlook's guard? When he brought Judith up here?"

"Who knows what either of them was thinking? Not about you, that's for sure. You were the last item on their agenda, that night. You didn't exist yet, for Judith. For Jim, you never existed at all."

It was such a stark truth — fierce, almost cruel. Hearing Mal say it, Beatrice knew precisely why they were here. She had to acknowledge it; not only that, she had to understand it. Her real father hadn't rejected her, by dying. He hadn't even known about her existence.

"Come on out," Mal invited. "You must see the view properly, especially tonight."

The evening air was still balmy, but she pulled her spare sweater on as he came round and opened her door. "Why especially tonight?"

"Wait a few seconds, then you'll see. Look — up there!"

She was standing on soft grass, leaning on the car, gazing up into this marvellous black canopy, embroidered with new stars in the new dark. Beatrice had never seen anything so intricate, so lavish, each individual pinprick a distinct colour. She saw whites, creams, silvers, golds, blues, greys, ochres, reds, even greens. She saw twinklings, glitterings, unblinkings and delicate winkings. She saw the powdery sweep of the Milky Way. She saw exactly what Judith must have seen, up there with Jim in this same spot, over two decades ago. A mere split second, in the scheme of the universe.

Mal had his arm around her shoulders, and with the other hand he was pointing to the sky.

"See the Big Dipper? And over

there — that's Scorpio rising. You wouldn't see that in England, this time of year. I know about Scorpio, because it's my birth sign, and as it happens, it was Renata's as well."

Beatrice was aware of this delicious shudder: a new sense of being alien, perhaps irresponsible — caught in a distant land where the night sky was different from at home. Then, as if Mal was orchestrating the heavens, came this final sanctifying touch: a shower of shooting stars, directly above their heads. "Did you see that?" she cried.

"I sure did." Mal was close beside her. "Catch a falling star, and put it in your pocket," he crooned. "We get a lot of meteorite showers, especially late summer. This one was performed early, for your benefit. They generally come on stage round midnight."

"You obviously have friends in high places!" She was still craning upwards; she could have gazed at it for ever.

"You ain't seen nothing yet. Take a

look over there — no, that way!"

In a lower part of the sky, the stars were fading even as they were appearing, where a brighter gleam outshone theirs. Brighter, and still brighter, a shimmering rim sliding into view over the horizon. Less silver than white gold, perfect curve swelling, so slowly, into a globe.

"She's going to be full, tonight," Mal commented.

Beatrice had to clear her throat, before she could speak. "Is that why you wanted to come here tonight, Mal? To see the full moon rising?"

"To show you the full moon rising from Overlook, Beatrice. I've seen it a dozen times, and I guess I'll see it a dozen times more."

"Oh, Mal!" There were tears in her eyes, so that the burgeoning moon wavered and warped, and she had to look away.

"Care to walk a few steps?" Mal took her hand, and they set off, their feet soundless on turf and night-scented heather. But with his next observation, he brought things down-to-earth with a bump. "Keep a watch out for poison ivy. Oh yeah, and the rattlesnakes."

Obligingly, Beatrice clutched his arm. "*Rattlesnakes?*"

He chuckled. "You're great, Beatrice, you know that?"

Beatrice withdrew her hand from his arm. "Are there really rattlesnakes?" she asked, a trifle haughtily.

"You'd better believe it. So, keep your shoes buttoned up — this is the brave new world, remember? You're up with the pioneers, here."

"It's not exactly the wild west," she muttered.

"I was serious about the poison ivy; I've known people badly stung. Depends how susceptible you are; I don't get much trouble from it."

Well, you wouldn't, she thought. "And the rattlesnakes?"

"They've been seen up here. I've never even heard one myself, but we'd better take no chances; stay close to me just in case, hey?"

His arm crept round her again, and she resigned herself to it, and its profound effects. The whole effect on her of the man himself: his presence, his mood, his incredible creativity in devising this event, for her sake . . . comprehending her unresolved needs, her empty spaces . . .

He steered them back towards the car, and as they strolled, he started talking again; but this time it was like a private poem, a litany — a sharing, a celebration of his beloved home territory.

"I've been in a lot of places, Beatrice, but I've never seen anywhere quite like the Catskills, and the Adirondacks. So much sun, on so many trees. So many trees, on so many hills. You should see them in the fall, when they're a mass of burnished red. And in winter, every peak solid white, streaked with sharp shadows."

"I hope I will," she murmured.

"I've watched the full moon rising

here." His voice was low, yet every syllable pierced her, clear as a chime. "And over the Shawangunk range, at New Paltz — near Mohonk. I've seen it set, over the Ashokan Reservoir. Listen to those names, Beatrice; you only have to say those names and you know you're in Indian country. You can see those guys, hear them, the natives who belong here, whose roots stretch deep down and centuries back before we Yanks burst on their scene . . . grabbed their land, covered it with log cabins . . . homes of wood, among their woods . . . "

She was so enthralled, she failed to notice when they reached the car. Mal stopped walking and talking, faced her, drew her to him. She didn't resist. There was a symbolism about this, after all: an inevitability; a levelling of the ground, before building could be done — or some basic negotiation, far more elemental than that? A crowning of this night, this mountain, this summer. Of simply being here: being Mal and being

Beatrice. Nothing of a past or a future; only this present.

His kiss was remarkably light and delicate — penetrating, while guarding its subtlety intact. Always those contradictions, keeping her guessing. Beatrice returned it at the same ambivalent level; yet she longed to open herself to him, throw all caution away; give herself up, for once in her life, to Mal, moonlight, magic.

His kiss deepened. Mouths fused, hands clasped, they sank down in the grass. Springy, slightly damp, it received them, rustling as they touched it. No poison ivy, no rattlesnakes, no other intrusive flora or fauna. Not even insects; just soft turf, soft night air, the Hudson Valley below, the cloak of stars with its moon brooch above.

And suddenly, it seemed, Mal's elaborate fortifications collapsed. In the confining city, in the privacy of his apartment, in his own wide luxurious bed, he had held back. Now, out here, on ground which belonged to no one, under sky which belonged to everyone, he let go.

Beatrice's final, half-conscious thought was to wonder why; whether it had something to do with beds being reserved for real relationships, such as his and Renata's, not fantasy ones . . . or with this place, being where he had brought Kerry . . . and where Judith and Jim had woven their spell which had resulted in Beatrice herself . . . then she, too, gave up, and gave way to the tidal wave of passion which engulfed them both.

Suddenly, after being so circumspect for so long, Mal became hungry to touch her, discover her, know her. In spite of her gathering responses, her own pent-up emotions, she struggled a little; glanced around them, exposed. When his mouth broke reluctantly from hers, it was smiling.

"Don't worry, Beatrice, I chose this spot carefully. It's well off the beaten track. No one else will come here, and if they do, when they see the car, they'll soon beat a retreat."

"What makes you so sure?"

"It's the unwritten law. I've lived here all my life, remember?"

She held him at arm's length, so that she could see into his face. "Mal? Why here? Why not — in bed?"

His smile faded, but his eyes shone, borrowing a warm bluish light from the moon. "I still wasn't ready for that. Were you?"

"I don't know . . . I thought . . . "

"Even if you thought you were, *I* wasn't. A time and place, right?"

"Yes, yes . . . you're right; I wasn't ready, not really . . . "

"We hardly knew who we were, did we, Beatrice? I hardly knew who I was myself, let alone who you were. Now, here, I feel I know myself better . . . and you much better . . . I know what I want, and I want this . . . I want this, with you, here, now . . . please, Beatrice?"

The floodtide rose again; this time they raised no barriers against it, so that it crashed over them in great breakers until they were formless, undivided — one single mass of sensation. Beatrice felt her precious singularity dissolve, and welcomed the feeling; felt herself tuned into that amazing grapevine, that network which mysteriously connected all the parts of her to each other, and to all of nature, and human nature.

Her responses were growing volcanic, but she surfaced enough to notice another paradox. The way Mal treated her body was wonderfully direct, uncompromising, toughly tender. Yet there was a reverence in the way he touched her skin: the way his hands ran through her hair, drew it back from her face, exulted in the shining texture of it. Sensing herself, through his fingers, she revelled in the experience, as if she was the outsider, exploring herself — meeting herself, making acquaintance with herself; nothing stale, everything shiny-new, superb.

The ground wasn't too damp, and it

was clean. The air was balmy, despite a light breeze. Mal was warm, gentle, yet rough and hard, emanating strength and vitality, virility. She wanted the man; how she wanted him! She held him in her grasp; she felt powerful, a spider-lady. Should she devour him, chew him up, suck all the goodness from him and spit out the husk, go her own sweet way to build the next web?

No, she would fill him up, replenish him, even as he was replenishing her. This was what it was all about: love.

Her eyes opened, and she stared straight up, past Mal, into that peppered dome of sky. As she stared, another shower of stars sprayed — a blessing? All would be well; whatever came of this union, it would be good. Images she carried away would be good. No product of this union could ever be anything other than totally good.

Had Judith felt the same, right here, so many years ago? In this moment Beatrice knew, beyond doubt, that she had. It was Mal's gift to her, that knowledge.

Mal pressed against her, as if the shooting stars had shot a new life-force into him. She opened her soul to accept him. He was totally with her, within her, and she had never known anything so sublime. She heard, as if from far away, her own voice crying, crying out to the enveloping night.

For a few seconds, the universe seemed to hold its breath. Then the stars and moon resumed their course, Beatrice opened her eyes, and Mal rolled neatly over, so that he lay on his back, and she rested on him.

"My turn for the lumpy bumpy ground," he muttered.

"It was all right, Mal . . . not too lumpy at all . . . really . . . " But it was good to feel a return to control, lift herself a few inches so that she could gaze into his illuminated face. "So much for bringing all those sleeping bags and things," she said.

"The best laid plans?" He grinned.

She smiled back. "It was exactly right, what you said about laying my private ghosts. No ghosts were ever so thoroughly dealt with . . . I could feel them calming down, understanding what we were there for . . . "

"That's great, Beatrice." He hugged her. "That's what I hoped."

"And you, Mal? What about you?"

"Me? Oh, I'm doing very nicely, thank you."

"You know what I mean. Your ghosts. Your . . . "

"Mine are a bit more complicated, maybe." He folded his hands behind his head, and contemplated the stars. "I don't know. I have one more to confront — one more major block to shift — then I'll know . . . "

"Here?"

"No, back home." He freed his hands, so that they could come up to frame her face, then slide down to her neck, her shoulders, her breasts. "Not that I'd be averse to a reprise, if that's what you had in mind."

"I didn't mean that . . . I meant . . ."

"I know. I mustn't be greedy; use you all up, now I've found you."

"There's plenty more of me where that came from, Mal."

"I believe there might be — for both of us." He smiled up at her, winding his fingers in her hair.

"We're mad, of course, you realise that?" she said, after a pause.

"Oh, I realise that."

"We were taking the most awful risk . . . apart from with our feelings . . ."

"I know; I figured we had to do that, so you could lay your ghost."

"You mean, I wouldn't have understood Judith and Jim, if we'd been more careful — the way they weren't?"

"I guess I mean that. Sometimes, life has to be a touch risky. If we want to learn from it."

"But Mal — suppose we . . . suppose I . . ."

"It might be kind of inconvenient, sure — but I can think of worse disasters than a child created by you and me, Beatrice. Can't you?"

"Good grief, Ma . . . " To be truthful, she could think of a million worse disasters; here and now, tightly enfolded in the firm warm grip of instinct, she could think of nothing more right, or splendid. Then she recovered her reason. "As it happens, it's extremely unlikely, if not impossible. That's not to say we shouldn't have been more . . . "

"I know."

"You know what?"

"I knew it was extremely unlikely. Don't look so scandalised — it's not such an invasion of your female privacy! I'm a grown man, and an observant one at that. I've kept company with you, day and night, for nearly a week. And I've lived with a woman long enough before; I know the score — the cycles. I read the signs."

She sighed, then laughed. "I don't know about you, Malcolm Cameron."

"You know as much about me,

Beatrice Cole, as I know about you, which is a lot, considering a week ago we didn't know each other existed."

She nestled against him. The breeze sharpened, bringing gooseflesh to the bare places of her skin. "It's getting cold," Mal said. "We should take you home to a nice cosy bed. We'll get rheumatics if we lie out here any longer, and I can't afford that — got to keep my fingers supple, or where's my bread and butter?"

"One nice cosy bed, Mal? Or two?"

He considered. "Does it matter? After this last hour?"

"I think it does," she said. "Doesn't it?"

"You're right, maybe it does. Okay, I tell you what, Beatrice. Share my bed if you like, tonight — I mean, I hope you will; I want you to. But there's this other hurdle I still have to go through — to put us through, tomorrow. Until that's out of the way, sleeping together will be exactly that, no more and no less."

"Like in New York?"

"Like in New York."

"And if this — hurdle . . . if it turns out to be okay after that?"

"After that," Mal said, "if it turns out okay, I shall gladly take you to my bed, as often as we both want, in the fullest sense."

"And — and if it doesn't? Turn out okay?"

"Then," he said, "I have to re-assess everything. Not just you, or you and me. Me, myself; what I'm ready for; what I'm doing with my life. Where you fit into that. Everything."

"I see." But Beatrice only wished she did. That rare after-glow was already fading, cooling to an irritating edge of anxiety. Stronger than that: fear. She was bewildered, but she knew there was no way he'd explain, even if she asked. She must get through this night, before she even found out.

And after she'd found out, suppose it turned out to be a catastrophe, whatever it was, and he sent her away;

decided he wasn't ready, that she had no place in his life after all?

The idea sickened her. Proof positive: she wanted to stay in Mal's life, more than she had ever wanted anything. And she wanted him to want it, too; not just to want her, like this; but to want that other, far more perilous, more elusive thing. A partnership. A commitment.

But there was nothing to be done except wait till tomorrow. She prised herself away from him, knelt on the earth for a few seconds, appreciating its solidity beneath her; then stood up and stretched.

"Come on, then, lazybones!" she said, as she sorted her clothes from his in the moonlight. "What are you lounging around for? I liked the sound of that cosy bed."

11

CONTRARY to the clear promise of the evening, next morning dawned grey and humid. Mal insisted on taking Beatrice out to breakfast at one of the local diners, despite the fact that neither of them had slept well, and Beatrice, at least, had little appetite.

"We're both going to need all our strength in a couple hours' time," he remarked — only adding to her general sense of unease.

In the end, Beatrice had opted to sleep alone, in Mal's spare room. Here, she had a double bed to herself: a normal-sized one this time, but still large by British standards. The window was wide open, complete with vital anti-insect screen, but she missed the Greenwich Village air-conditioning. In the small hours, the atmosphere had become oppressively muggy, and much darker, as clouds obscured that glorious moon. Beatrice's breath had grown shallow, her throat tight, her pulse fast, as anxiety took its cruel nocturnal grip.

Outside, she could hear cicadas, owls, frogs: all those comforting country-night noises which reminded her of another country night, spent tucked up with Mal in a double sleeping bag not a hundred yards from where she lay now.

It was incredible — ridiculous — the way her feelings for the man had developed since then! Then, they had hovered on a threshold. Now, they had well and truly crossed over, so that there was no ambiguity, not a shred of doubt about them. She knew they were set to last; would never change, unless forced to . . . at this moment her future was in the balance, depending on . . .

On what? On whatever mysterious test Mal planned to spring on them both in the morning. Tomorrow would be the first day of the rest of their lives; a good chunk of them, at least. But lives spent together — or apart?

Her mind went on churning through counter-arguments, emotions, fears, expectations until, around five, she finally dozed off. Only to be woken at eight by Mal, bearing a glass of freshly-squeezed orange juice, and raring to get on with the morning. Typical Cameron; having reached his decision, there would be no shilly-shallying.

Externally he seemed unruffled, but over breakfast, his inner stress became only too obvious to Beatrice. Demolishing a stack of pancakes with bacon and maple syrup, washed down with black coffee, his usual verbal control deserted him. He rambled and gesticulated, treating her to a stream of impersonal monologue. It was bemusing, but at least all she had to do was keep her own apprehension at bay and keep listening, offering occasional encouraging comments of the "is that so?" variety.

She watched him carefully, as she sipped her coffee and toyed with a slice of cinnamon toast. He was a man in an acute state of conflict, that much was evident. She guessed he was struggling to reach another decision — perhaps his most crucial one yet. One of those critical personal watersheds, which must be faced here and now, or the moment will be gone. Of course it was largely about her — but she suspected not entirely, even if their mutual future hung upon it.

There was little of the personal in what he was actually saying to her at this moment. With a supreme effort, because she sensed how important it was to Mal, she focused all her concentration upon it.

He was describing a place, not far from Woodstock; this sculpture park, a massive project created by one man and known as Opus Forty because it had been designed to take forty years to complete. Mal seemed strangely hyped up about it, but Beatrice suspected a symbolic level here: he was talking about it, yet not really talking about it at all.

At last he fell silent, gazing expectantly across the table at her. Some real response was called for.

"And did this Harvey, er. . . "

"Fite. I told you, I knew him by sight, back in the 'seventies, when I first started being interested in sculpture — of course he was years older than me."

"And *did* he finish the project in forty years?"

"Beatrice, haven't you been listening to me? I said, he died before the time was up. Three years short of the forty, must have been around 1976. In an accident, right there on the site; fell under some piece of his own machinery. But he almost finished it. There wasn't much more he could have wanted to do. It was all there — statues, pools, ramps, fountains, this amazing obelisk at the centre . . . "

Beatrice's imagination was engaged,

in spite of her own stretched nerves. "How sad — that he never lived to enjoy it, or see other people enjoy it, except while he was building it!"

"Sad?" Mal growled. "I guess so. But what a way to go, hey? A man could hope to die that way, suddenly, doing his best work. As for seeing it enjoyed — that's exactly my point, Beatrice! That's what I'm always asking myself, especially . . . well, especially now. *Is* that what he wanted? How did he plan for it to be used — appreciated? Was it all for his own benefit, or was it right that it should be shared with the rest of us poor mortals who might not have his talent or vision?"

He was fierce, waving his fork at her, brow heavily furrowed. Whatever troubled him so deeply — whatever it was she had to help with — this was near the nub of it. One thing Beatrice was sure of: they weren't simply discussing this Harvey Fite.

She was cautious, but she knew she must state an opinion, for Mal's sake.

"If he bought the quarry specially," she said, "and made this — this edifice out of stone he found there . . . "

"Bluestone," he interrupted. "Lovely stuff."

"Well, surely he must have intended to make a public show out of it. What else would he do: keep it all to himself?"

"Or blow the whole goddarn shooting-match to kingdom come," Mal said, "once he got it the way he liked it."

"Mal! Don't be stupid! That's a terrible idea!"

"Not so stupid as all that, Beatrice. Do we work for our own sakes, or other people's, that's my question?"

She considered. "I should say," she said, "it depends on whether we do it for a living or not."

Mal chewed and swallowed and drank, staring away from her. She thought she had lost him, and then, quite unexpectedly, he grinned. "I should have known you'd take the practical view, woman. Whatever we do, we do it because we have to eat, right?"

"I didn't quite say that. Of course I know there's more to it than that. My mother's an artist, remember?"

"Of course I remember." He leaned across the table. "I remember a whole lot about your mother. For someone I've never met, I feel I know her remarkably well. We have some interesting common concerns, Judith Cole and I. You, to name but a few."

Beatrice dropped her gaze to her plate, colouring. His sudden slip into intimacy was more challenging, if anything, than all that artistic soul-searching.

"Perhaps we could go and see Opus Forty sometime," she muttered.

"You'd like that?"

"*If* you would," she said.

"I go quite often. No reason why you shouldn't come with me — some time." It was non-committal, but apparently the best she was going to get. And he left her no time to answer, because now he was pushing back his plate, getting to his feet, reaching for his wallet.

"Ready to go back?"

"Yes, I'm ready."

She followed in his wake, as he paid and strode out to his car. They drove the five minutes to his house in fraught silence. Whether all that breakfast chat had been part of today's big test or not, Beatrice had no way of knowing. Nor whether, if it had, they had passed to the next grade.

The instant the car was parked, Mal was out, slamming his door, marching across his lawn, and summoning her, over his shoulder. Once again, his mind was made up and he needed to act. She finally reached him as he unlocked and unbolted his workshop, then charged in, like some armed police raid apprehending a heist.

Beatrice hesitated, vividly recalling the last time she'd stood there. So recent, so different! That time, he had barred her entrance — denying her so much as a glimpse of what lay within. He had made it all too plain how unwelcome she was, here in his holy of holies. Now, he was flinging the door wide, actually commanding her to enter.

She stepped gingerly inside. Her sandals crunched on rubble. Dust flew up, disturbed by Mal's stampeding boots, to settle on her bare arms and legs, in the creases of her cotton dress. She had to shut her mouth, afraid to breathe in case she inhaled any of it. It stung her eyes, so she briefly closed them as well.

But he was still charging ahead, still beckoning to her, past the scattered debris, sad half-completed carvings — or had they been completed, then roughly broken up? — past all those trolleys and pulleys and tools; disappearing through another door, into an adjoining room.

With rising perplexity, picking her way, Beatrice followed. The new space, the inner sanctum, opened up in front of her. Slightly smaller — but what a contrast! Where that space had been stuffy, choked with grit and grime, redolent of extreme distress, this one exuded a rare tranquillity. It was clean, cool. It contained no smashed lumps of stone, no rubble. No dust, even. In fact it was empty — apart from one, towering piece, alone on its pedestal at the centre.

It loomed, twice the size of its creator as he stood next to it, one hand laid against its side, palm flat as if he would like to merge with his own creation. His eyes, harder, colder than the stone itself, were steady on Beatrice. He said nothing, and neither did she, but she approached, bravely, slowly. When she was near enough to see it in detail, yet still in total, she halted.

It was pure white, the virgin density of limestone newly shaved and shaped, its surface pockmarked with chisel-scars. She was no artist, but she recognised a piece of work finished in form, but not yet smoothed, polished for presentation.

If, that was, Mal ever intended to present it?

Then it percolated through: the relevance, the point of that cryptic breakfast conversation! This was Mal's therapy, performed over these last anguished months, by himself, on himself, for himself. But did it have anything to offer the rest of the world? Did he *want* to share it with the rest of the world?

The rest of the world was here with him now, as represented by Beatrice. He was experimenting, with her. She was the first and only person whom he had trusted, since his cruel loss — enough to open this intensely private, painful place, reveal this chunk of himself. Upon her verdict, her response — above all, his response to her response — would hang not only the future of this devastating creation; but her own future, and his.

The challenge was so daunting,

Beatrice was momentarily pole-axed. How could she go through with it?

Then she rallied. Mal stood, as still as the stone, waiting. She surveyed him, the human subject, for several seconds; then transferred her full attention to the object, the extension of its maker. Which was exactly what it was, of course: an extension of Mal. One level of her had known all along, and now she gazed her confirmation.

It was an enormous self-portrait, lifelike, yet hugely beyond life, with that overpowering head, massive shoulders, a trunk like an ancient oak tree. A ferociously thrusting beard, so intricate that she could distinguish every wiry curl. On the head, too, strands of hair writhed like hissing snakes.

A furious frown on the wide white brow; such cracks, such crevices, etched an inch into the stone! Equally deep lines running down from bleak eyes, jutting nose, to tormented mouth. More lines all around the mouth, which was so finely carved, Beatrice had to bite the inside of her own lips to prevent a cry of compassionate pain from escaping.

Tears burned her eyes; she blinked them back. On whose account did she feel such pity: her own? Mal's? The human race's in general? Just then, it would have been impossible to separate them. The man and this image, his alter ego, were one; and both were one with Beatrice and the whole of suffering mankind.

Had she said the room felt tranquil! Not so! The air was rent with wails and sobs. They burst from the statue, filling each corner, up to the lofty rafters. You needed no special artistic sensitivity for them to reach you; they assaulted you, whether you invited them to or not.

She couldn't blame him, fearing to share this with the rest of the world. The need to guard it, protect it, surely cut both ways: for his own sake, a natural reluctance to expose such a raw slice of his soul; and for the sake of anyone witnessing it. You needed a strong spirit to withstand such an impact. Once you'd seen this, you wouldn't forget or recover in a hurry. It was four-dimensional; it was five.

She knew Mal was observing her every flicker and flutter. When he assessed that she had had as much as she could take, he tore his hand from his creation, painfully, as if the flesh had grafted itself there in those few minutes. Then, without a glance back at it, he walked away — holding that same hand out to Beatrice.

She feared to take it, in case it scorched her, but she followed. Out through the partition door, back into the confused chaos of the outer studio; through that, fending off those terrible tortured resonances — far worse than those of the statue, because they were unformed, anarchic — and at last, gratefully, outside again.

Only then did she accept his extended hand. It was cold, even in this heat, and grasped hers very tight, fingers threading and twining with hers. His expression was curiously calm, but quizzical.

She couldn't seem to locate a single word. Mal was the first to speak. "Are you all right, Beatrice?" was what he said.

She nodded. Just then, the sun emerged from behind its cloudbank — and strangely, perhaps because Mal's eyes were fixed upon it, she became aware of her cap of fair hair, full of its own life, gleaming, dancing.

"That was a mean trick to play on you," he said.

"No, Mal." She was husky, but at least she found her voice. "No, I understood. I understand."

"No other person has seen that. That's what's used up all my time, all my energy, these past eight months. All day, every day, many nights too — until last week, when I was distracted," he added, with the hint of a grin.

"I believe you," she said.

"The thing is, Beatrice . . . " He jabbed a finger into his chest. "This is me — but so is that! Which is the real me, that's the problem?"

"Couldn't it be both?"

He mused, and she waited, scarcely breathing.

"You're right! Dead right. As I made it, I felt it — all that misery you saw in there — shifting into the stone. Not out of me altogether, but finding a home there. Stone has the permanence, the durability, the hardness to take it. I don't."

"I do see. I understand." The sun invaded her eyes, and thawed her skin from clammy-cool to warm, and now hot. But Mal was staring at her expectantly, and she knew she must be bold, express her own reactions. It wouldn't be too difficult, since she was in no doubt as to what they were. "I think it's fantastic, Mal! It's the most amazing thing I've ever seen in my life. I think you were right to share it with me, and I feel privileged that you did. And I really do understand, because — well, I just do, from knowing you, being with you . . . " *loving you*, she was on the point of saying, but curbed the impulse just in time. "And standing in there with you just now," she went on, "seeing you, you and it together, anyone would understand exactly what it's about, what it means . . . of course they would."

"Of course they wouldn't," he said.

"What?"

"No way, Beatrice. Not just anyone."

"You don't think so?"

"I know so. What's more, I'm not even sure I want them to! That hunk of limestone isn't just a piece by Cameron. It *is* Cameron. So who wants to display all that to the world, hey? Their innermost self, their deepest loss, their bitterness . . . "

"But Mal, surely that's what art is all about?" Beatrice felt humble, being an outsider to that magical process; but she knew her own opinion.

"Maybe so. Maybe I should share that — that other me with the rest of poor benighted humanity. So, you think I shouldn't go back in there, pick up the nearest sledgehammer, shatter that thing into tiny fragments, after all?"

"No! No, please don't do that, Mal!" Suddenly, she had forgotten all about tests and hurdles and the significance of this whole event for herself; her place in his life. All she could think of was Mal's work, his statue, what it meant to him and about him; and the tragedy, the sheer appalling waste if it was destroyed. "You must — you've got to share it," she implored, moving closer to him, one arm outstretched. "When it's finished!"

"You can tell it's not finished?"

"I can tell it's nearly finished. I can tell it's not completely ready, and you're not completely ready to let it go public. When you both are, you'll know, and then — well, then I think you should share it. The world deserves to see it. It deserves to be seen."

He reached out and took her outstretched hand. "And when — or if — I'm ready, and it's ready," he said, softly, "do you realise you'll be partly responsible for that?"

"I — I . . . if you say so, Mal." She stared down at their linked hands.

"I say so. And then, Beatrice, after that — what do you think? Do you think you'll have done your job in my life? That I'll be finished with my need for you, rehabilitated, so we can both go our separate ways?"

This was the crunch, of course; the burning question. How could she bear it? How could she reply? She looked up, into his face. It was positively bland, compared with its agonised portrait in the workshop. It gave nothing away. "It's up to you," she murmured, "but . . . but I hope not," she added, more firmly.

"You do?"

"Yes, I do. I don't want to lose you, now I've found you. I — I love you, Mal. I think your work is wonderful, but that has nothing to do with my feelings for you. I love you, the man, the person you are — that's all. I'm sorry, I've probably got it all wrong, said all the wrong things, I never meant to . . . Oh God, I'm . . . "

She broke free, wrenching her hand from his so that she could brush away the idiot tears. She turned and fled, but he caught her from behind, swung her round, pushed her against the wall of his workshop, and imprisoned her there, one arm either side of her shoulders, his face close to hers.

"Don't you dare be sorry! Don't you dare say that to me, any more!"

"I'm sorry, I . . . "

"You haven't said any of the wrong things, Beatrice. You've said all the right ones. From the moment I first set eyes on you, you've said, and done, everything just right, as far as I'm concerned. What you felt, and said, about — that feller in there . . . " Unwilling to release Beatrice from the secure confinement of his arms, he jerked an elbow at his workshop, " . . . was what I hoped you'd feel, and say. As it happens, I agree with every word. But that wasn't the point."

"No?" She gulped, coasting this wave of shock, and a dawning joy.

"The point was, I took a major risk in showing you at all. Not just with your feelings — that was delicate enough — but with mine. I had to see how *I'd* feel, letting you in there . . . opening that door to you . . . "

"And you felt . . . ?"

"Fine. It felt perfectly natural. You have a natural response, an instinctive wisdom, and you care, and I found I wanted you to be in there with me, seeing it. But up to then — believe me, Beatrice — I was afraid! I was so afraid I'd regret it, the moment we walked through that door. I should have known better. I should have known you better, trusted my feelings for you better. It's been so long since I trusted my feelings — or had any to trust . . . "

It was his turn to falter; for his voice to crack, his eyes to cloud.

"I know, Mal — I know!" Her

arms came up, spontaneously, winding round his neck; and then his were round her, warm about her back, no longer a prison but a haven. "Poor Mal . . . poor Mal . . . you've had such a rough time!"

"I'm not the only one. You've been so strong, Beatrice. You don't know how much I've admired you — your spirit — coming all this way, searching for roots you only just learned you had . . . taking it on the chin when you found out the worst . . . if there was ever going to be another woman for me, I thought to myself when I met you, this would be her!"

"You really thought that?" Beatrice gazed up at him in wonder.

"I really did. When Renata died . . . " He swallowed hard, but looked her in the eyes as he continued. "I never thought I'd love again. Now, I know I can . . . I will." He gathered her into his arms once more. "I do," he muttered, into her neck. "Already do. Oh, it won't be the same — how can two loves ever be the same? New person, new set of feelings. Not second best — just second. But it'll be there, Beatrice, no question — if you give it time . . . give me a little time, and it'll be there. For as long as you want it."

"Oh, Mal!"

"We could make a great life together!" His exuberance, once released, was infectious. "We could we could stay in my apartment while you're studying in New York, and come back here vacations, weekends, whenever we can. It'll suit me fine — I need to be with someone — with you; and I need to expand, spend more time there, see folk again. I need to get back in the circuit. What do you say, Beatrice?"

"I say . . . " She hesitated, but she was smiling. Her deliberation was not through uncertainty; she was simply relishing the pure delight of his delight — and of what she was hearing. "I say yes, Mal. Yes!"

"Beatrice!"

Lost for words, he picked her up

bodily, and swung her in the air. Then he put her down, gently, and took her hand. In step, they set off across the lawn.

As they went, Beatrice raised one final puzzle. "Mal, if that's all you've got in your workshop — where's the rest of your work?"

"Oh, didn't I tell you? I rent this other workshop in the city, and I store most of my stuff there — whatever isn't in private vaults, homes, galleries, exhibitions. Just as well," he added, tersely, "or there wouldn't be much left of it now.

"All that mess in there . . . was that . . . "

"That was all the pieces Renata and I were currently working on, when she died."

"And you broke them up, when you heard?"

"That's right. Pulverised every last one of them. That was my one-man earthquake — my Malquake. Now you mention it, I guess it's time I got tidying up in there. Clear the decks. Get that outer studio back into some kind of shape, ready for action."

"Can I help you do that?"

They had reached the house, and stopped outside, face to face, no longer touching.

"You've already helped me more than you'll ever know, Beatrice."

"No more than you've helped me," she pointed out.

"And I dare say we'll be giving each other a lot more help, one way and another, before we're much older," he said. "But — don't be offended — that's one job I guess I'll have to do for myself — by myself."

Beatrice nodded her complete comprehension.

"You haven't managed to offend me yet, Mal," she said, "so you're not likely to start now."

Then she smiled, and reached for his hand again; and together they went into the house.